# Living in the Truth

I0627912

Book Two of *The Truth and Lies*
Five-Part Series

## Demetrice Nichele

*Living in the Truth*
Copyright 2018, 2023 by Demetrice Nichele.
All rights reserved.

This is a work of fiction. Names, characters, business, events and incidents are the products of the author's imagination. Any resemblance to actual persons, living or dead, or actual events is purely coincidental.

Published by TJS Publishing House
PO Box 2382
Matthews, NC 28106
www.tjspublishinghouse.com
contact@tjspublishinghouse.com

Published in the United States of America
ISBN: 978-1-952833-38-0
ISBN-13: 1-952833-38-8
Fiction / African American / Romance
Fiction/African American/Suspense

# ACKNOWLEDGMENTS

I've been working on this book for a long time, and I could not have gotten it done without the strength of God. I have to thank him for this blessing and the blessings to come.

Next, I would like to thank my best friend who is like a sister to me, Petrina Winston. I love our weekly conversations about life, with you living on the west coast, while I'm on the east coast. We've been friends since the fourth grade, and no matter where we live and how much time goes by between our visits; we have always been able to maintain our close friendship for forty-years. During one of our many conversations about life, you encouraged me to write a book. You reminded me of how much I used to write while in grade school. Thank you so much for reminding me of this gift. You are and have always been a great friend to me.

I would like to thank my children, Kyia Jones and Tyshon Prezzy. You both are my heartbeats, and I am proud to say that you have grown to be genuinely good people. Thank you for always supporting and encouraging me in whatever I set out to do.

Next is my editor, Shameka Daughtry, who is also my sister. Thank you so much for taking the time to read my very, *very* rough draft and correcting all of my errors, helping me to make it into a story that everyone can enjoy and understand. You are an awesome editor and sister!

Thank you also to my wonderful and funny publishing consultant Tonya Edmond Joyner of Tonya Joyner Speaks. She came in at the end, formatting and pulling everything together for me and it has been a blessing.

Last, but definitely not least, are my supporters: Tekia Williams, Michelle Prezzy, Cheryl Daughtry, and Shirley Bray-Sledge. Thank you all for reading my book before it was published, giving me your input, and encouraging me to move forward. Also, to my Aunt Queen Mitchell, thank you for always having my back and being there always. To Sharon Battle, thanks for the endless love and support, pushing me to get this book finished and published.

If I have left anyone out, please forgive me. I do love and appreciate you, also. Please charge it to my head and not my heart.

# CHAPTER 1

Charles stood still, holding the pregnancy test in his hand, looking at Yvette. He wasn't sure what she was trying to tell him. Even though he was holding the test in his hand, it wasn't registering.

Yvette stood with her hands on her hips, looking like she was enjoying this moment. She laughed, walked up, and stood in front of Sam. "What's wrong, Charles? A cat's got your tongue?"

Sam finally found his voice. "Yvette, I don't understand. We always used protection, and you were supposed to be on the pill."

Yvette rolled her eyes. "With everything going on, I never gave it a second thought. You stressed me out so much that I barely remembered to eat on some days."

Charles took a deep breath, sat down on the stairs and held his head in his hands. He couldn't believe that this was happening-- *this could not be happening.*

As if reading his thoughts, Yvette walked over and sat down beside him. "Yes, Charles, you have another baby on the way. Wait until Daddy finds out you got both of his daughters pregnant. He's going to have a stroke. You have succeeded in single-handedly embarrassing and ruining my family's reputation."

Charles stood up and looked down at Yvette. "So, I guess you have already decided what you're going to do."

Yvette laughed. "I'm keeping our child, Charles. And know this. You will take care of us. If you thought I was going to get rid of our child so you can go on with your happy life with Tessa, then you've lost your fucking mind. I'm having this baby, and I don't give a fuck what anyone has to say about it! I am going to see a lawyer to see what my rights are as the mother of your child. If you're smart, you'll take my advice and not piss me off any more than you already have because I could make your life very miserable."

Charles stared at Yvette and shook his head. He didn't know what to believe. She was so conniving and sneaky. "I tell you what, Yvette, call and schedule a doctor's appointment, and I'll go with you. If you are indeed pregnant, I will do what I have to do for my child. I will also see my lawyer to find out my rights and to put something in place to support the baby."

Yvette stood up and walked towards the door. "Fine. I'll text you the appointment information, seeing as you're having a problem believing me. I have no problem with that because you will take care of us, and you will be in this child's life." With that being said, Yvette walked out of the door and slammed it shut behind her. She needed to make her exit before he decided to question the paternity. He had no reason to because, as far as he was concerned, she was busy trying to figure out how to keep him and not running into the arms of another man for comfort. The truth of the matter was that she didn't know if the baby was his or David's, but she knew that David couldn't give her the type of life she and her baby deserved. Charles would take care of them, and she wouldn't have to work.

Charles felt like his head was going to explode. How the hell did he allow all of this to happen? What was he going to do? He had finally gotten Tessa back and was on his way to living a happy life with her and the baby-- now Yvette comes up pregnant. He knew he had to tell Tessa, but he was going to wait until Yvette's pregnancy was confirmed by the doctor.

# CHAPTER 2

Tessa could not believe her eyes. She was standing face to face with the man that physically abused her.

David looked at her with an evil grin on his face as if he was enjoying the moment. "Tessa, long time no see. I would ask what you've been up to, but I can see for myself."

Tessa seemed to snap out of her trance at the sound of his voice. She stepped back and tried to close the door. David was too fast for her and stuck his foot in the door, pushing it back open. Tessa stepped back and turned around to run towards her phone but stopped cold in her tracks at the sound of his voice. "I wouldn't do that if I was you. I can kill you and your bastard child right now, and no one would even know who done it."

Tessa grabbed her stomach and turned around to see that he was pointing a gun at her. Tessa began to rub her belly but could not seem to say anything. She just knew she and her baby were about to die. David walked over to her, still pointing the gun at her.

He stood in front of her, held up his hand, and began to stroke her face. Tessa closed her eyes and began to pray silently, not moving. David leaned down and spoke softly in her ear, "Tee, don't be scared of me. I never wanted to hurt you. You made me do those things to you. We could have still been together. You fucked shit up. I'm a felon. Can't get a job or nothing. And here you are, all happy with a booming business and about to be a mother. You even got you a man who loves you. But that nigga ain't me."

"He don't know how to handle your big ass. But it's all good. I'm about to even the score between us."

Tessa looked at David, and she felt her eyes begin to water. "David, please don't harm my baby. It's innocent. Please don't do this. If you leave now, I promise I won't tell anyone you were here. Just don't harm my baby. Please, I will do whatever you want."

David laughed, an evil glint shining in his dark eyes. "You bet you gonna do whatever I want. I have the upper hand here. Now grab your purse and phone, and let's get out of here before your man gets back."

Tessa immediately panicked. "Where are we going? Please, David, I'm begging you. What is it that you want? Money?"

David became angry and slapped Tessa with his free hand. "Bitch, you don't have enough money to repay me for ruining my life! Get your shit, and let's go." Tessa fell over on the couch from the impact of the blow. She grabbed her face and began to cry. She stood up while rubbing her stomach in an effort to calm down her baby. It felt like the baby was doing flips inside of her.

"Okay, David, I'll do whatever you say." She walked to her bedroom with David walking closely behind her with the gun sticking into her back. Her mind raced, trying to figure out how to leave a clue for Sam-- or even better, a way to escape. She could not think of anything, nor could she stop the tears from falling.

She grabbed her purse and her phone off her nightstand and headed towards the door. David was right on her tail.

They approached her front door, and David stopped her. "I am going to walk beside you with my arm around your shoulders." He grabbed her and put his arm around her. She felt a poke from the gun in her side, and her body began to shake. She had no idea how she was going to get away from him before he killed her and the baby.

They walked outside, and she looked around for anyone to help her. David grabbed her tightly and nudged her to walk down the street. "We're going to get in that white van a few houses down. Don't try to be funny, Tee. I will shoot you without giving it a second thought. You understand?" Tessa nodded her head, indicating she understood. Just as they made it to the van, she heard someone call out her name. She turned around, and it was Rome.

Rome looked at her curiously and started to walk toward her. "Hey, Tessa, did Sam call you? He told me to pick you up because he was stuck in traffic, and he didn't want you to have to wait too much longer for him." Tessa looked at Rome, but she could not speak. She felt the pressure from the gun in her side, and she felt her legs about to give out on her.

David took it upon himself to handle the situation. "What's up, man? I'm Tessa's cousin, and her people sent me to pick her up because Sam was taking too long."

Rome looked at David, then at Tessa, who looked like she had been crying. "Tessa, are you okay?" He started to walk towards them to get a closer look at Tessa. Something wasn't right.

Just as Tessa saw him walking towards her, she took all her strength and elbowed David in his side and began to run towards Rome. This caught David off guard for a second, and he dropped the gun.

Unfortunately for Tessa, it wasn't long enough. He quickly picked up his gun and shot Tessa in her back. Rome ran to Tessa as she hit the ground.

David saw Rome running towards them and began to shoot some more. This time he aimed at Rome. Rome felt a burning pain in his shoulder, but he kept running towards Tessa. David jumped in the van and took off.

Rome got to Tessa, who was lying on her stomach. Blood was everywhere. He rolled her over, not even paying attention to his own wound.

Tessa wasn't moving, and he couldn't tell if she was breathing. By now, Tessa's neighbors had come out and were surrounding them both. Rome cradled Tessa's head while screaming at those surrounding them. "Someone call the fucking ambulance! She's been shot, and she's pregnant! I don't think she is breathing!"

...

Sam raced to the hospital-- he prayed that Tessa, the baby, and Rome would be okay. He just could not imagine who would do something like this. He asked Rome to pick up Tessa, as traffic was terrible on the way from Norfolk. He didn't want Tessa to have to wait much longer since she had been waiting for him for hours already. He figured it would kill time for Rome to pick her up and meet him.

Now, he was racing to MCV Hospital in Richmond because his girlfriend and his best friend had been shot, and no one had any idea who had done it.

Sam raced into the ICU and saw Tessa's parents sitting and waiting-- along with the Duncans, Angela, and her husband. Just as he walked in, the Duncans walked up and hugged him. He hugged the Grants and Angela as well.

"How is she?"

Elizabeth Grant looked at him and sobbed. "Where were you, Sam? You were supposed to pick my baby up. How did she end up shot down in the street along with your friend?"

Sam immediately felt guilty. It seemed like he was the cause of all of Tessa's pain, but this was the worst. "Mrs. Grant, I am so sorry. I had an issue to take care of beforehand, and then I was stuck in traffic. I sent

Rome to pick her up to save time, but I don't know what went wrong. I haven't talked to Rome. I came straight to the ICU. How is she and the baby?"

Mr. Grant walked over to Sam and put his hand on Sam's shoulder. "Son, it's not looking good. Tessa was shot in the back-- she lost a lot of blood, and the baby lost a lot of oxygen. They're in surgery right now. All we can do is pray." Sam sat down, held his head in his hands, and began to cry quietly.

This could not be happening to him again. He just could not lose Tessa and the baby.

Mr. Duncan sat beside Sam and tried to comfort him. He knew how Sam felt. Sam had already lost his parents and his aunt, they were the only blood relatives he had, and now there was a chance that he might lose his baby.

The older man placed his arm around his mentee's shoulder and consoled the only son he had ever had. Sam leaned into Ed Duncan and began to cry. Ed Duncan began to cry, as well. This started a wave, and everyone began to cry.

Ed Duncan finally found his voice. "Son, let's go find Rome to make sure he is okay. It's nothing we can do right now-- it's all in God's hands."

Mr. Grant stood up. "I think I'll come along. I need to know what happened."

Rome sat up in the hospital bed and finished up his conversation with the detectives. He suffered a gunshot in his shoulder-- the bullet was a through and through. He was fortunate that it was also just a flesh wound. He had to stay in the hospital overnight for observation and would be free to go home tomorrow. Even though he was happy about the status of his injury, he was still worried about Tessa. He felt worse because he didn't do anything to prevent her from getting shot. He had been asking the nurses about her condition, but he was told they could not disclose any information to him about her.

"Dude, I'm so glad to see you sitting up and talking. Are you okay?" Sam rushed over to his friend and gave him a hug. Sam was so happy to see that Rome was alright.

Rome smiled at his best friend. He was happy to see him, but then again, he was sad that he didn't save the mother of his child. "Yeah, man, I'm good. It was just a flesh wound. What about Tessa and the baby? Nobody will tell me shit around here!"

Sam sat down on the side of his friend's bed-- Rome only now noticed how tired his friend looked. "They're operating on her right now; they're trying to save them both. That's all we know for now. All we can do is pray."

A tear rolled down Sam's cheek. Rome really felt bad about this whole thing.

Mr. Grant cleared his throat-- walking over, he held out his hand to shake Rome's hand. "I'm George, Tessa's father. What happened?" Rome shook the older man's hand and gave him a sad look. Ed Duncan walked over and gave Rome a hug, as well. Rome took a deep breath and began to recall the whole incident again, just as he told the detectives.

"Sam called me and asked me to pick up Tessa for him because he had been dealing with some things that took more time than he anticipated. He knew he had to get her to the shower by a certain time, so he thought it would save time if I picked her up and met him with her at the mall because he had a surprise for her. When I pulled up, I saw Tessa walking towards this van with this dark-skinned buff dude. I thought it was strange because he had his arm tightly around her. I got out and called Tessa. She turned around, and I told her I was there to pick her up. She never said a word."

"The dude spoke up, saying he was a cousin and her parents sent him to pick her up. When I looked at Tessa, she looked scared and like she had been crying. I started walking towards them. I mean, the shit just didn't look right. Before I knew it, Tessa had pushed dude or something, and she started running toward me. Man, it all happened so fast. The dude was bent over, but when he stood up, I heard a pop, and Tessa went down. I started running toward them, and I heard more shots rang out, but I kept running.

"He jumped in the van and drove off. I ran over to Tessa, and she wasn't moving, man, and there was blood everywhere! I held her head and just called her name, hoping she would open her eyes. The paramedics came and took us both to the hospital. That's all I know. I don't know who dude was-- he was buff, dark-complexioned, and he had a skull cap pulled down on his eyes. I just wish I had gotten there earlier or acted faster. Maybe he wouldn't have shot her."

Mr. Grant put his hand on Rome's arm. "Son, I'm glad you came when you did. It sounds like he was trying to kidnap Tessa, and if you wouldn't have showed up when you did, who knows what could have happened? By your description, it sounds like it could have been…" Mr.Grant paused, thinking. "No, it can't be. He's in prison."

Sam looked at George, puzzled and asked, "Who are you talking about, Mr. G?"

Mr. Grant shook his head. "It almost sounds like David. That thug Tessa used to date and had arrested because he started hitting her."

Ed Duncan spoke up. "I thought that fool was in prison-- and if they released him, they were supposed to contact Tessa."

George nodded his head in agreement. Sam's phone went off-- it was Angela texting. Tessa was out of surgery.

# CHAPTER 3

Yvette had been blowing up David's phone for the past two hours. He wasn't answering or returning her calls. She had no idea what was going on. She was becoming nervous.

According to the plan, he would make Tessa disappear, and she would handle Charles. She didn't tell David about the baby because she didn't know how he would feel about it or how it would affect their plan. Now she was getting nervous because she hadn't heard from him, and the time for the baby shower to start had passed.

She called her mother to see if she was still at the baby shower and to get some information, but she didn't pick up. She called her father-- he picked up on the first ring. She tried to sound normal. "Hey, Daddy."

Her father cut her off before she could say anything else. "Baby, we're at the hospital. Something terrible has happened to Tessa and the baby. Try to get to MCV hospital as soon as you can." Before Yvette could respond, he disconnected the call.

Yvette stood up and began pacing back and forth. Her stomach was in knots. What could have happened? Didn't David finish the job? Where was he? She really needed to get to Richmond and the hospital to find out what was going on. Just as she grabbed her keys, her phone rang. She picked it up. There was an unfamiliar number showing.

"Yo, I need some cash. I need to lay low for a while."

Yvette felt angry and relieved at the same time. "David, what the hell happened? What is she doing in the hospital?"

David spoke in a whisper. "I can't go into detail. I need you to meet me at our first spot and give me some cash. I'm hot right now."

Yvette felt sick to her stomach. This was not going according to plan. She needed to get to the hospital to find out what was going on, so she and David could figure out their next move. She knew she needed to get some cash to him, but she just didn't have access to any at the moment. That was all going to come into play once Charles confirmed her pregnancy with her doctor.

"Yo! You still there?"

Yvette jumped at the sound of his voice. "You know my situation. I don't have much cash right now. I--"

"Well, you better figure it out because I think that bitch is dead."

Yvette felt herself panicking. "No, I just spoke to Daddy. They're at the hospital. I'm on my way to

Richmond to the hospital. I'll figure out what's going on. Sit tight, and I will call you back at this number."

David spoke low and deep, "Don't fuck me over, Yvette."

Yvette felt a chill go through her body. "David, I got you. We're in this together." David didn't respond. He just disconnected the call. Yvette grabbed her purse and keys and hurried out the door to Richmond.

# CHAPTER 4

Elizabeth and George Grant held hands while waiting anxiously for the doctor to update them on their daughter's condition. The Duncans sat patiently, along with Angela, her husband, and Sam. Dr. Walker stood with a serious look on his face. This is the part of his job that he hated.

"Well, as you know, your daughter suffered a gunshot wound in her back. While she was lucky that the bullet missed her spine, it traveled through her back, and the bullet hit the baby."

Elizabeth cried out. "Oh my God, no!" Sam, Angie, and the Duncans began to cry.

The doctor continued. "We tried our best to save both of them, but we could not save the baby. He wasn't strong enough to endure the impact of the bullet or the trauma of the surgery. I am so sorry to have to bring you this news. We did everything we could. Tessa is alive, but she is in a coma. We will keep her comfortable, but the rest is up to her-- as the operation was so intense, the recovery pain, along with the loss of the baby, might be too much for her right now. You can go in and see her two at a time, but you can only stay for a little while. Does anyone have any questions for me? I know this is a lot to take in at one time, and there was no easy way to tell you."

Elizabeth was the first to speak. "Will Tessa be able to walk?"

Nodding his head, the doctor answered, "Tessa should be able to make a full recovery physically, but I am concerned about her mental state. This whole thing is very traumatic, and I think she will need extensive psychological treatment. If there is nothing else, the nurse will come out and let you guys know when you can go in."

Sam stood up, "Doctor, what about my son's body?"

Dr. Walker turned and looked at Sam with sorrow in his eyes. "They're in the process of cleaning up his body. I advised them to wrap him in a blanket so you won't have the trauma of seeing the gunshot wound, but you will be able to see his face. Again, I am so sorry."

Sam stood with his head down, crying. How could this be happening to him-- he knows he did wrong with Tessa and Yvette, but he was trying to make things right.

Maggie walked over and put her arms around Sam. "Charlie, sometimes we can't make sense of the Lord's will. We just have to trust him. I know this is hard, but you have to be strong for Tessa. She is going to need you more than ever when she wakes up."

Sam nodded his head and agreed. "It just hurts so badly. He was an innocent baby. He didn't even have a chance to…" Sam started to cry again.

He wanted to get away. He needed to get away. He made his way down the hallway and out of the hospital. Ed got up to go after him, but his wife stopped him. "Give him some time to get his thoughts together. He will be back."

Yvette walked into the hospital and was directed to the ICU. She informed them that Tessa was her sister, and they immediately let her in. She walked down the corridor and found her parents holding each other while crying. She walked over to them, and she noticed Angela and a handsome man holding each other, as well. Her parents realized she had arrived and grabbed her and gave her a long hard hug. She pulled back and looked at the both of them. Their eyes were swollen, and they looked tired and haggard. She immediately felt jealous that they had all of this emotion over Tessa.

"How is she?" Her father just shook his head and walked away. He needed some air, and he wanted to find Sam.

Her mother took her hand and answered her. "She lost the baby, Vette. The baby is dead."

Yvette tried to show some emotion, "Oh my God, Mommy! What in the world happened?"

Her mother put her arm around her daughter. "Apparently, her ex-boyfriend showed up at her house with a gun and tried to kidnap her. Rome showed up just before he got her in the van, Tessa tried to run away, and he shot her and Rome."

Yvette felt herself getting faint, and the room was starting to spin. She grabbed her mother's arm to keep her balance. Margaret grabbed her daughter and looked at her curiously.

"Vette, are you okay? Come over here and have a seat, baby."

Yvette allowed her mother to lead her to the chair, and she sat down. "I'm okay, Mama. It's just so much to take in."

Maggie looked at her daughter with concern. "Are you sure? You look pale, baby."

Maggie pulled a bottle of water out of her bag and handed it to her daughter. Yvette gratefully took the water and turned it up to her mouth. "Thanks, Mommy. I'm okay now."

Sam and Ed Duncan came walking back down the corridor. Sam stopped and noticed Yvette sitting next to her mother. He looked at her but didn't say anything. He was in no mood to deal with her right now. She got up to try to say something to him, but her mother stopped her. "Let him be, Vette. Give him space." Yvette sat back down and obeyed her mother.

# CHAPTER 5

Sam walked into the room and immediately wanted to cry again. Tessa looked so weak with all of those tubes coming out of her body. All kinds of machines were beeping-- it was all unreal to him.

He walked over, kissed her lips, and held her hand. He pulled the chair up close to her bed, sat down, and stared at her. The tears would not stop, but he didn't care. "Tess, baby, I am so sorry this happened. I was trying so hard to make sure that you were happy, but it seems like I failed both you and our son. I just want you to wake up and be okay, baby. I don't care about anything else. I will be here day and night until you wake up, get well, and get out of here. I will never put you in anyone else's hands again." Sam broke down and cried again. "I have to go see our son and tell him goodbye. This will probably be the hardest thing I will have to do in my life, but I just need to see his little face and hold his little hand to let him know that his Daddy loves him very much and will always love him. I just need to hold him one time, Tess. He needs his Daddy to hold him."

Sam put his head down on the bed rail and began to weep. Mr. Duncan walked in and put his hand on Sam's shoulder. "Charlie, the baby's body is ready." Sam stood up and followed Ed out of the room. The baby was placed in a room so the family could all say their goodbyes to him. He was wrapped up in a blue blanket. The nurse handed him to Sam first. Sam held him closely and kissed him on his forehead. He still felt warm. He reached into the blanket and pulled out his little hand, and kissed it.

"Little man, your Mommy and I never had a chance to discuss names. But I'm sure we were going to name you Charles Samuel Thompson Jr. I just wanted to hold you, one-time, little man. Daddy loves you and will love you forever. Your grandma, grandad, and Aunt Hannah will take care of you up there. You won't be alone. Don't worry about Mommy. I'm going to take care of her." Sam held the baby close to his chest and could not stop crying. Ed walked in and took the baby from him and handed him to the nurse. He ushered Sam out of the room. Sam looked at Ed Duncan and wiped his eyes. "I want to find this David to see if he did this to my family."

Ed looked at Sam. "Charlie, I feel the same way, but we have to be rational about this thing and let the police handle it. George already spoke to the detective and told him what he knew. The detective looked him up and found out that he was released a year ago, but they failed to inform Tessa. Now, we have to give them a chance to do their jobs and not get in their way. I'll tell you what, I have a PI friend that I deal with from time to time. Let me get in touch with him and see what he can find out to help the police along, but only to help with the investigation. Not for us to take matters into our own hands. I already lost my grandson. I refuse to lose you or anyone else in my family."

Sam agreed to drop it for now. "I'm going to stay here with Tess. You guys can go home and get some rest if you like. I'm not leaving."

Elizabeth Grant stood by Sam. "I'm not leaving either. Sam and I will be fine. We will look out for each other. You all can go home and get some rest. If there is a change, we'll call y'all."

Angie stood up and walked over to her mother and took her hand. "Are you sure, Mommy? I can stay, too."

Elizabeth gave her daughter a hug. "I'm sure, baby. You go explain to those girls what happened to their auntie and their little cousin. I'm sure they will have plenty of questions."

Angie smiled at her mom and gave her another hug. She hugged Sam tightly and whispered softly in his ear. "Call me if you need me. Remember that you are not alone." Sam kissed her on the cheek and smiled.

After Angela and her husband left, Yvette walked up to Elizabeth. "I'm Yvette. I'm sorry we have to meet under these circumstances, but I just wanted to give you my condolences and tell you how sorry I am that this has happened to Tessa." Elizabeth looked at Yvette strangely, but she gave her a sad smile and thanked her. Yvette gave Sam a weird look and walked away.

Elizabeth watched her walk down the corridor. She couldn't help but feel that there was something off about that girl. She gave off bad energy, and Elizabeth was never wrong about a person's energy. She made a mental note to watch her closely whenever she was around.

# CHAPTER 6

Yvette got into her car, and her cell phone rang. When she answered, she heard David's voice on the other end. "Yo, what you find out?"

Yvette rolled her eyes. He had totally fucked up the plan, and now he was looking for her to pick up the pieces. "David, you shot her and killed the baby! And you shot his best friend, Rome!" She could hear him cursing under his breath.

"Well, that nigga don't know me, but I need to get out of town before she wakes up and tell them I did it."

Yvette shook her head. "They already know you did it. The guy you shot gave a description, and her father named you."

David began to panic. "What the fuck?! They are probably looking for me right now! Yo, you gotta bring me some cash right now! If I go down, you go down with me!"

Yvette began to think. "Look, I don't have any cash right now. I have some jewelry, and my mother has a lot that she won't even notice is missing. They are all up at the hospital. Let me run home and get the jewelry, and you can pawn it in the morning or something. That's the best I can do."

David was pissed. "No, you can do better than that! I'm not pawning shit! I just told you I'm hot! You pawn that shit, and I'll call you tomorrow so we can meet. That will help me get out of town, and you better come up with more to keep me gone because if I have to come back, you won't be happy." Once again, before she responded, he had disconnected the call. She jumped on the highway and headed towards Norfolk.

What had her life come to? First, she loses her fiancé to another woman-- a woman who turns out to be her sister. Her parents cut her off financially, and she gets pregnant by a thug who turns out to be a murderer. Not to mention the fact that she was an accessory to a murder, and now she was about to go steal from her mother. What had her life come to? And it was all because of Charles and Tessa.

Yvette pulled up to her parents' house and felt anxious. She really did not want to steal from her parents, but at the moment, there was no other way. She figured once Charles started paying child support for the baby, she would have the cash to send to David to keep him hidden and get her parents' jewelry back. She knew the baby was his. She always had protected sex with Charles. Even when she was seducing him after the whole thing with Tessa, she always made sure her birth control was in place. She had unprotected sex with David when she first started going to his house.

She hadn't expected to have sex with him, and when she realized that it was going to be the norm with them, she began to take her birth control before going to see him, but by then, it was too late. The damage had already been done. If things go according to plan, Charles would never question the paternity of the baby. This is why she had to make sure David disappeared. With him gone, no one would connect her to him.

She walked into her parents' home and went up to their bedroom. She took a deep breath before she went into her mother's closet, where the safe was stored. She entered the combination and opened the safe. Her mother had so many diamond bracelets and earrings. Her father always spoiled her with them, and her mother wasn't the type to wear bling, so she stored her diamonds in the safe, keeping them to pass down to her children and grandchildren.

Yvette grabbed three diamond bracelets and two pairs of earrings that her mother never wore and hurried out of her parents' bedroom. Yvette entered her bedroom and went into the safe that contained her jewelry. She had accumulated several pieces from her parents, boyfriends, and Charles over the years. She never thought in a million years that she would be going through something like this, but desperate times called for desperate measures. She needed to make sure that David stayed gone, and there was no other way. She gathered all of her jewelry, including the engagement ring Charles had given her along with the wedding set they purchased and put it all in a Louis Vuitton duffle bag with the jewelry she had taken from her parent's safe. Yvette sat on the floor and began to cry-- her life was suddenly so overwhelming.

Her phone began to vibrate, startling her. She realized she was sleeping on the floor. "I must have dozed off," she mumbled to herself as she reached for her phone. She didn't even bother to look at the caller ID before she pressed talk. It was David on the other end.

"Yo, did you come up with anything?" Yvette felt her chest begin to tighten up. She really needed a drink but decided against it, considering her condition.

She breathed into the phone and spoke in a low tone. "Yes, I have everything, and I'm going to take care of it in the morning."

David breathed heavily into the phone. "Good. I will call you in the morning with a location. Make sure you act normal and keep yo mouth shut, and everything will be fine. I know this wasn't the plan, but plans change." Yvette sat quietly on the phone as tears ran down her face. She didn't want him to hear her cry and make him think she was weak. David noticed her mood. "Look, Mama. I can't have you freaking out on me right now. Remember, if I go down, we both go down. Now, let's do what we said we were going to do and keep it moving. No time for second thoughts. You are in too deep. Remember, you started all of this."

Yvette felt a chill go down her body that made her shiver. She held the phone to her ear and closed her eyes as she spoke into the phone in a low tone. "I'm cool. I just don't want to say too much over the phone or in my parent's house."

David wasn't convinced, but he had to take her word for right now. She was his only hope at the moment. "Ok, that's cool. I will hit you up tomorrow morning."

Yvette heard the phone disconnect, and a voice behind her startled her. "Vette, why are you sitting on the floor? Are you okay?"

Yvette turned around and saw her mother standing in her doorway, looking concerned. She quickly zipped up the duffle bag and stood up and smiled at her mom. "Yes, Mommy, I'm fine. I thought I dropped my earring, and I was looking for it."

Maggie looked at her daughter curiously and walked up to her to look into her eyes. "Vette, what is going on with you? And don't try to run no game on me. I'm not your Daddy. I understand this whole situation is a lot to take in, but you have been very distant and quiet, and that's not you at all."

Yvette stepped back from her mother and began to panic. She could never fool her mother. She wanted to tell her about the baby, but now was not a good time because their focus was on Tessa. But what better time to spill the beans? Everyone was so busy worrying about Tessa and Charles. What about her? Yvette cleared her throat and tried to speak, but nothing came out. Tears rolled down her cheeks, and her mother took her in her arms and held her tightly. Yvette broke down, and her mother held her even tighter. "Vette, no matter what the situation is, and no matter what is going on, I'm still your mother, and I love you no matter what. I know there's a lot going on, and you may feel pushed aside, but trust me when I say your daddy and I are just as worried about you, too. You won't talk to us, and if you don't talk to us, we can't help you. There isn't ever anything so bad that you can't come to us about it. You may not like what we have to say about it, but we will make sure we do what is best to help you."

Yvette held her mother and cried harder, but she did not say a word. Maggie pulled away from her daughter and looked her in the eyes again before she kissed her on her forehead and led her into her bathroom. She directed her daughter to undress while she ran her a hot bath. Yvette obeyed her mom. She felt like she had no strength left in her. When she was undressed, she stepped into the tub and let the bubbles and hot water take control of her body.

Her mother got a washcloth, sat on the side of the bathtub, and proceeded to wash her daughter's back. She used to do this for her when she was younger if Vette was sick or upset about something.

Yvette closed her eyes and enjoyed her mother's attention. It felt like old times. She never wanted this moment to end, but she knew it would, and it would be back to reality.

# CHAPTER 7

Sam sat in the chair next to Tessa's bed. He had been at her bedside for three days, and Tessa had not awakened. The nurses felt so sorry for him that they let him shower in the employee's quarters. Rome had been bringing him a change of clothes every day. Each day, he called Detective Mason to find out if there were any leads on finding David, but there hadn't been any. They checked with all of his relatives, his known hangouts and had a detective posted outside of his mother's house just in case he showed up. They really needed Tessa to wake up to see if she could provide any additional information.

"Sam, you really should go home and get some rest. I will be fine with Tessa for a few hours. They have an officer posted outside her door. She is safe."

Sam looked up and smiled at Angela. "I'm good, Angie. I want to be here just in case." Angie looked at Sam and felt so bad for him. She knew how he felt. She wanted her sister to wake up, but then again, she didn't want her to. Then, she would have to suffer the news of losing her baby. She couldn't imagine losing one of her babies. She hurt so badly for her sister. She couldn't understand why David would appear after all of this time to do something like this. He was released a year ago. Why would he wait until now to do this? Something was just not adding up if it was him who really did this to her.

Charles's cell phone went off, and he looked at it and frowned. It was Yvette. "Hey, hold on a second."

With everything going on with Tessa and their baby, he had forgotten all about their situation. He looked at Angie and stood up. "Um, Angie, I have to take this call, but I will be right down the hall if you need me."

Angie looked at him and smiled. "Take your time."

He walked out the door and put the phone back to his ear. "Yeah, Yvette."

Yvette laughed. "Well, hello to you, too."

Charles rolled his eyes. He really didn't have the patience for her right now. "Yvette, you know I am going through some serious shit right now. Damn! Where is your heart? She is your sister no matter what the situation is."

Yvette sucked her teeth. "Look, I didn't call to talk about her or the shit you're going through with her. I have my own shit to worry about like me having a baby all by myself. I have an appointment tomorrow at 10 am. You will get the confirmation you need so badly."

Sam sighed into the phone. He didn't want to leave Tessa for long, but he knew that Yvette was a loose cannon and he had to be easy with her, as this whole situation was delicate. "I will be there. Just send me the address."

Yvette sounded pleased. "Okay, and once you get the confirmation, we can start discussing the future of our child." She disconnected the call.

Sam leaned against the wall. He felt a headache coming. He also felt a huge storm coming, and he didn't know how to take cover.

# CHAPTER 8

Yvette sat at her desk in her father's office and went online to browse the online fashions at Nordstrom for maternity clothing. She knew if she was patient and let things die down while waiting for Tessa to heal, she would get Charles back one way or another. He had no blood relatives, and as far as he was concerned, she was carrying his only heir. She weighed her options about telling David. If she stayed away from him, sent him money, and only talked to him on the phone, he wouldn't find out about the pregnancy and cause problems. Most likely, since he was on the run, he wouldn't anyway because he didn't want to resurface and go to jail.

She had gone back and forth so much in her mind about this whole situation that it had given her a headache. She felt nervous all the time. She jumped each time her phone went off, and she barely made eye contact with her parents. She knew she had to be careful around her mom because she was smart, and she knew her better than she knew herself. That really annoyed her.

Her phone vibrated, and she sighed because she knew it was David. For someone who wanted to lay low, he called her constantly. She answered and rolled her eyes. "Hey."

David seemed to be in good spirits. He should. After all, she was about to meet him and give him thirty thousand dollars in cash. She was upset because that jewelry was worth a lot more than that. "Hey Mama, what you doing?"

Yvette frowned. What did he want now? "I'm at my father's office, working. What's going on?"

David spoke in a low tone. "What's wrong? You sound upset or something. Did anything happen?"

Yvette tried to cheer up. The last thing she needed was for him to become paranoid or suspicious of her. "No, I just have a headache. I haven't been getting a lot of rest."

David sighed and spoke in a low sexy tone. "That's cause you're missing this good dick you love so much. Tell you what, I'm going to call you back in a few hours and give you some information so you can meet me. I want to see your sexy, bourgeois ass. And bring some Henny with you, along with the cash. I got all the other stuff."

Yvette became annoyed. How could he think about sex and getting high after he had just killed a baby? She tried to put him off. "I really have a lot going on today, so I won't be able to stay with you for long... My mother wants me to have dinner with them, and like I said, I have this headache--"

"I didn't ask you all of that. I said come see me and give me some pussy. I'll call you later with the details." As usual, he disconnected the call before she could respond. Yvette felt like throwing her phone across the room. She wished she could run away.

Her father walked in just as she was about to put her head down to have a good cry. He walked over to her and gave her a kiss on her forehead. His wife told him about the other night, and he felt awful, but he didn't know what to do to help his baby girl.

"Hey baby, what you have going on today?" Yvette gave her dad a weak smile and made sure she clicked off the website she was surfing.

"Hi, Daddy. I thought I would go hang out with Erica tonight." Erica had been her best friend since grade school. She married straight out of college to a doctor she met in Dubai when they were on a family vacation. She hadn't really spoken to her since she informed her that she would not be able to make it to Yvette's wedding because she had her baby prematurely and couldn't travel so soon. Erica was back in Virginia and had been blowing up her phone so they could get together.

Ed looked pleased that she was going to hang out with her childhood best friend. "That's great, baby. I saw her dad at the country club, and he told me she was in town. That will be good for you." Yvette smiled and stood up to leave. "I'd better get home so I can change and head on out to her parents' house." Ed waited for her, put his arm around her, and they walked out of the office together.

# CHAPTER 9

Sam walked back into Tessa's room and almost walked right into Angie. She looked up at Sam nervously. "I was just about to come get you. She is awake and asking questions. I'm about to get the nurse."

Sam rushed over to Tessa's side. "Hey, baby, I'm so glad you're awake."

Tessa gave Sam a look of confusion and tried to speak again, but her voice was very hoarse. "Sam."

Sam gently placed his finger on her lips. "Shh...baby, don't try to talk. Wait for the doctor."

Just as she was going to try to speak again, the doctor and two nurses hurried into the room. They asked Angie and Sam to wait in the hallway while they examined her.

Angie and Sam didn't want to leave, but they did. Once they were in the hallway, Angie called her parents, and Sam called Ed and Maggie. Both couples were overjoyed and on their way to the hospital. Sam began to pace back and forth, and Angie sat down. "Sam, have a seat. We have to brace ourselves for what's to come."

Sam sat next to Angie and put his head in his hands. He wished that this was all a bad dream. After what seemed like an eternity, the doctor walked back out into the hallway to join them. Just as he was about to fill them in on Tessa's condition, Mr. and Mrs. Grant came rushing down the hallway.

Once they were all together, he cleared his throat and began to explain Tessa's condition. "Tessa is awake. We had increased her dosage of pain medication. Even though she is awake, she is not out of the woods. She will need to go to physical therapy to strengthen the muscles in her legs and back. Also, she is going to need some counseling once she receives the news about the baby. Right now, she is asking for you guys, and she is demanding to know what happened, meaning she doesn't remember, or she is blocking it out. Either way, we will have to keep a close watch on her. I will notify the detectives that she is awake, but she doesn't remember anything at this moment. We have to take one day at a time. Her recovery all depends on her. You all can go to see her now, and I will stay close by to monitor her once you all tell her about the baby. It's hard to say, at this point, what her reaction may be." Everyone thanked the doctor and hurried in to see Tessa.

When they all entered, Tessa was busy trying to get the nurse to tell her what had happened to her. She looked up when she noticed all of them standing in the doorway, staring at her.

Her mother was the first to run over to her, crying and hugging her. "Tessa, baby, I'm so glad you're awake." Her father walked up with tears in his eyes and leaned down and hugged his daughter. Angela walked over and kissed and hugged her sister as well.

Sam waited patiently for her family to finish showing her love. He was so glad she was awake and talking. His eyes began to water looking at Tessa-- he had never loved a woman so much. Tessa looked across the room, and their eyes locked. Sam smiled at her and walked over to her. He leaned in, hugged her, and kissed her all over her face. He didn't care that her parents were present.

All of a sudden, as if Sam was a sudden reminder, she placed her hand on her stomach. She frowned and looked at Sam and put her hand on his cheek. "Is this the reason I'm in here? Did I have the baby?"

The room suddenly became silent. Sam looked back at her parents for help. They walked over and stood by Sam. Tessa frowned again, "Why is everyone looking so crazy? Where is my baby?"

Sam grabbed Tessa's hand and began to speak. Besides burying his son, this was going to be the hardest thing he had to do. "Tess, baby, there was an incident, and the baby, our baby, didn't make it, sweetie." Tessa looked at Sam and then at her parents and sister.

She looked back at Sam with tears in her eyes and hit him on his arm. "Sam, that's not funny! Now go get our baby!"

Sam felt the tears, and he couldn't stop them. Mrs. Grant tried to help Sam out. "Tessa, baby, unfortunately, Sam is not joking. Someone hurt you and--"

"No, Mommy! No! Somebody get my baby!" Elizabeth went over to her daughter and put her arms around her. Tessa pulled away and tried to get up-- she felt the worst pain shoot in her back, and she let out a loud scream. The officer and nurses came running into the room to see what was going on. Sam tried to comfort Tessa, but she would not stop screaming. The nurse ran back out and came back with a needle and injected the medication into her IV, and Tessa began to calm down. Her screams lowered to a whimper. The doctor walked in and asked them all to step out for a few minutes.

They all walked back into the hallway, shaking and crying. The Duncans walked up, looked at their expressions, and didn't have to ask what was going on. Ed Duncan walked over and gave Sam a hug. Maggie came over and did the same. They'd known Sam for most of his life, and they knew this was tearing him apart.

The doctor walked back out, and they gathered around, waiting for him to speak. He took his glasses off as he spoke. "We gave Tessa something to calm her down, but I didn't want it to knock her out. I know there is no gentle way to tell her what happened to her, but I think it all may be coming back to her. She is asking for you guys to come back in."

"I checked her vitals, and her blood pressure has gone up, but that's to be expected considering what she is going through. I'm going to ask for only one of you to stay with her tonight, and I'm going to put in a call for the psychologist to come to see her tomorrow. She will also start physical therapy tomorrow with the approval of the psychologist. She needs to get started on her physical recovery as soon as possible in order for her nerves and muscles to heal.

Mr. Duncan was the first to speak up. "Won't that be a bit much considering her mental state right now, doctor?"

The doctor shook his head. "The sooner, the better. She can't lay there and stiffen up. She needs to stay busy instead of lying in bed thinking."

The nurse walked out of the room. "She is asking for Sam." Sam hurried back into the room while the others waited outside. They knew they needed time alone.

Sam walked over to Tessa, sat on the side of her bed, and held her hand. She looked so tired and sad. His heart hurt so much for her. She was groggy from the meds, but she spoke anyway. "Was it a boy or a girl?"

Sam spoke softly, looking away. "A boy, Tessa. We had a son."

Tessa began to cry. "Sam, I am so sorry. I shouldn't have opened the door. I thought it was you at the door. I should have fought him, but he had a gun. I didn't want him to hurt the baby. And when I saw Rome, I just knew it was my chance to get away. I elbowed him with everything I had and ran. Now I'm here. Did he shoot me? Sam? Did I fall and hurt the baby? What happened after that? I don't remember! I don't remember, and our son is dead! Oh, God-- my baby! He didn't deserve this! He was an innocent baby! I should have died! Not my baby! He was supposed to live!"

Tessa began to rub her stomach and looked at Sam. "Where is he? I want to see him, Sam. I want to see our son."

Sam looked at Tessa. He wasn't sure if she was in the condition to do that right now. He wasn't even sure if he was in the condition to see him again. "Tess, I will have to check with your doctor. I'm not sure how this will work. You can barely move."

Tessa started to cry. "Sam, please get them to let me see him. I have to see him, Sam. They have him in that morgue, cold and alone. I need to see my baby, Sam. Oh God, how am I going to live without him?" She screamed and cried some more.

Sam began to cry and put his arms around her. "Tess, I'm here for you. We have each other, baby. Just let it out. I know it hurts."

Tessa stopped crying and looked at Sam. "Sam, please forgive me. I am so sorry I didn't protect him. I let him get killed. I'm so sorry, Sam. I didn't mean it. I tried to save him, Sam. Honestly, Sam, I really did try. I really and truly tried."

Tessa cried uncontrollably. Sam felt like his heart was breaking into a million pieces. He didn't know what to do. The pain was too much. All he could do was hold her and cry with her. "Tessa, baby, I know you tried, I know. It wasn't your fault, baby. I should have come straight to Richmond instead of going to check on that house."

Sam thought about that every day since this happened. If only he hadn't gone to the house, his baby would still be alive. Tessa sniffed and buried her face in Sam's neck while she spoke. "Take me to him, Sam. Take me to our son."

# CHAPTER 10

Yvette walked into her room and lay on her bed. She was so tired, mentally and physically. She had the house to herself. Her parents had rushed off to the hospital. Her stomach felt like it was in knots. She needed David to call her. She didn't know what number to contact him at because every time he called; it was from a blocked number. She needed to get this money to him and try to distance herself from him somehow. Her phone vibrated, and she jumped up and looked at the screen. It was Erica.

She decided to answer since she had been ignoring her best friend's calls. "Hey, stranger! Welcome back!" Yvette tried to sound as cheerful as possible.

Erica laughed and responded. "Hey, Diva! It's about time you answered my calls! I was starting to get offended!"

Yvette smiled. She really missed her bestie. She was like a sister to her. They kept each other's secrets and did everything together. They graduated from the same college, and both majored in marketing. Erica came from a wealthy family as well. Her father was a successful surgeon, and her mom was a socialite.

Though they were really close, they had different tastes in men. Erica loved thugs, but she didn't marry one.

She married a doctor named Phillip Townsend, who was 20 years her senior. He was a prominent doctor with a practice in Dubai. They met the summer her family and the Duncans took a family trip to Dubai. She met him at the hotel. He was recently divorced and decided to move to Dubai and open up a practice. One look at Erica, and he instantly fell in love with her.

Erica Collins-Townsend was a beautiful woman. She had a caramel complexion with hazel almond-shaped eyes, compliments of her biracial mother. She had curly sandy blonde hair that she wore in wild curls, which gave her an exotic look. She had an hourglass figure and was not ashamed to flaunt it. Erica was very beautiful and had no problem getting attention from both sexes. She always loved the bad boys, and it surprised Yvette when she started having this long-distance relationship with this older professional man.

Erica told her that she wanted to have her own money and not depend on her parents. She also wanted to have a lavish lifestyle. Though she loved the bad boys, she knew they could not afford the lifestyle she was used to. Erica announced one day that she and Phillip were getting married, and they had a big lavish wedding.

Yvette had to admit she was a bit jealous. So she'd put pressure on Charles to marry her, insinuating that her parents expected it. When he gave in, it made being happy for her friend easier, even though she was moving far away. She was going to miss her partner in crime like crazy. She was even more upset when Erica told her she couldn't make it to her wedding because of her pregnancy. She really missed her friend and needed her to be there.

When everything happened and the wedding was called off, she didn't even bother to call Erica. She was too embarrassed. She figured Erica certainly knew by now since their mothers were very good friends and their parents hung out all the time. Erica tried to call her, but she was not in the mood to talk about it.

Now that her bestie was back in town, she was actually glad. She needed someone to vent to who would support her. Erica was just the person she could talk to without worrying about judgment. She was hoping married life had not changed her. Yvette put her phone on speaker as she undressed to get ready for a bath. This baby really drained her. "Don't be offended. I have just been going through a lot. You know I still love you."

Erica laughed. "Okay, good, because I was feeling some type of way. I've been home for a week, and I haven't even talked to you. Nor have you come to see your goddaughter."

Yvette stopped in her tracks at the mention of Erica's baby. She rubbed her stomach and sighed.

"Don't worry, girl. I'm about to take a bath, change, and pack a bag. We will pull an all-nighter, and I will spoil my god baby, Faith. With so much going on, I haven't even had a chance to go shopping for her."

Erica responded. "My mom told me about all the drama that's been going on with your family. I'm so sorry, Diva. Why didn't you call me? You could have even come to Dubai to escape from everything."

Yvette smiled. She really loved Erica. "I just didn't want to talk about it, Erica. It was one thing after another, and it still keeps coming. It's like it's never-ending."

Erica yelled. "What now, Diva? You hurry up and get over here, Yvette. I will have the wine and snacks ready."

Yvette sighed. "Okay, I will be there shortly." Just as Yvette was about to walk out the door, her phone vibrated again. She looked at her phone and saw that it was a blocked number, meaning it was David. She pressed talk and answered.

"Hey." She picked up her bags and headed out the door.

David spoke quietly into the phone. "Hey, are you alone?"

Yvette walked outside and to her car. "Yes. I'm alone. I'm on my way to my friend's. She just got back into town, and I am going to spend the night with her."

David wasn't pleased. "How the fuck you gonna do that when you're supposed to be meeting me?"

Yvette spoke quickly to calm him down. "I will leave her house to meet you and then go back, David. I have to appear as normal as possible. She is my best friend, and she's been gone for two years. I have to go and spend time with her. With Tessa being awake and all, you don't know what she has told the police."

David calmed down a little. "Okay, well, I'm going to send you the address to where I'm staying. You need to be there by midnight. I have to move at night to be on the safe side. Don't be late, Yvette. We have a lot to discuss. Try to talk to your parents before you come; see what you can find out. Call me when you're outside, and I will let you know the room number."

Yvette spoke softly. "Okay, I will. See you later." David disconnected the call.

Yvette started her car and started her journey to Erica's parents' house. She was so tired, but she was glad her friend was home. She really needed someone to talk to.

# CHAPTER 11

Erica disconnected her call with Yvette, and she smiled to herself. She was so happy she was finally going to spend some time with her bestie. They had so much catching up to do. When Erica left for Dubai two years ago, they promised to talk every day, but that didn't happen. So much had gone on in both of their lives. She was just glad to be back home and away from Phil so she could have some time to think.

She walked into her bedroom to check on Faith. She looked in the crib her parents had purchased for her and smiled down at her beautiful baby. At six months old, Faith was beginning to take on more features of both Erica and her father. She possessed Erica's sandy brown curly hair and caramel complexion, but she had her father's pointed nose and blue eyes.

Phil was a 59-year-old Caucasian man. They met while they were both at the pool at the hotel in Dubai. Phil kept staring at her, and she loved the attention of the handsome older white man. For a 59-year-old, he looked great. He was well built, with curly salt and pepper hair. He came over and introduced himself, and they hit it off immediately. He told her he was a physician that had just moved to Dubai from California and was opening up a practice. He hung out with her and Yvette the whole time they were there and treated them like royalty.

They spent a few nights alone and had sex. Though it wasn't the best, Erica did not write him off. She actually enjoyed her time with him. This surprised Yvette and her parents because she usually dated thugs. Once the vacation was over, he and Erica continued to talk, and she was making trips to Dubai to see him. They carried on a long-distance relationship for six-months before Phil decided he wanted to marry her. She accepted, and they planned a wedding where they spared no expense. Her parents were skeptical about their union because of the age difference, race difference, and the fact that Erica would be moving to Dubai with someone they barely knew. They couldn't say much because she was 29 years old at the time. So, they gave her their blessing.

After the wedding, they went to Dubai to start their life together. Phil immediately started pressuring her to have a baby because of his age. He wanted to be able to do things with his child. Erica wanted to wait for them to get used to being married to each other, and she wanted to adjust to living in a new country. Phil reluctantly agreed and said they would try in a year.

During that year, she tried to get him to try different things sexually, but he refused. That was when she started to get to know the real Dr. Phillip Townsend. After she had the baby, he became physically and emotionally abusive. On many occasions, he felt it necessary to slap and grab on her if he felt like she was getting, as he put it, *sassy with him.*

He had started popping Viagra and wanting to have rough, degrading sex with her. He even called her the "N-word" on several occasions during their rough lovemaking. She had started trying to figure out ways to get away from him. He also became very controlling when it came to the way she dressed. Erica had a great body, and she loved to show it off. He told her that her way of dressing was frowned upon in Dubai and she would embarrass him. He also didn't like to take her out dancing at clubs. He was always too tired, and since she had no friends, she didn't want to go alone. All his married friends were around his age, and Erica had no common interests with their wives.

When he told Erica he wanted to have a baby, she was skeptical at first because she felt so alone there. Things already weren't going the way she wanted in their marriage. She reluctantly agreed and got pregnant with Faith a year after they were married. Her pregnancy was hard because she was lonely and depressed, and he was not sympathetic to her feelings of loneliness and depression. She called her mom every day, and she wanted to talk to Yvette, but she could hardly get her on the phone.

During the pregnancy, she began to notice the change in Phil. He barely touched her, and he did not take her out. Not that she wanted to have sex with him. When he did feel the need to, he would get on top of her or behind her, and pump into her a few times, grunt, come inside her, roll over, and go to sleep. She became lonely and frustrated; she wanted to go home. She talked to Phil about going home when the baby was old enough to travel, and he agreed. All of a sudden, he told her that he sensed that she might be homesick, and he was sure her parents wanted to see the baby.

In Erica's mind, she had no intention of returning to Dubai. She also wondered what suddenly made him care about her feelings. She didn't have long to wonder. One night, they were invited to a dinner party by one of his colleagues. They took the baby with them because she didn't really trust strangers with Faith. During the party, she noticed that her husband had disappeared, but didn't think anything of it. Faith became fussy-- she needed a diaper change. The maid directed her to one of the guest rooms in the spacious home to change Faith. When she walked in, she was shocked to see her husband sitting on the edge of the bed and his colleague's 21-year-old daughter on her knees, between his legs, sucking his dick.

Phil's head was thrown back, and his eyes were closed. He was enjoying it so much that he hadn't even heard her walk into the room. Aminah, the girl who was performing on Phil, noticed them and jumped up in shock. That's when Phil opened his eyes to find out why she stopped. "Oh, shit! Erica!" Erica looked at him and smiled her most evil smile, and walked back out of the room clutching her crying baby. She walked out of the house, got on her phone, and called their driver.

While waiting outside, Phil came walking out of the door and approached her. "Erica, what were you doing in that room? You followed me?"

Erica looked up at her husband as if she was really seeing him for the first time, and she didn't like what she was seeing. "No, Phil. I was shown to that room to change our daughter. Does Dr. Assar know that you have his daughter sucking your dick?"

Phil got close to her and spoke in a low tone. "You listen to me, you black bitch, you're going to walk back in that party with my daughter and act like you're enjoying yourself. We can discuss this matter when we get home."

Erica looked at him and hissed. "No, you look here, you old ass, nasty white motherfucker! If I walk back in there, it's not going to be pretty! I suggest you get the fuck out of my face and go back in there with your friends. I don't give a fuck what you tell them about why I left. I'm sure you don't want to be embarrassed."

Phil backed up, and his face turned red. He stared at her for a minute and whispered. "You go home, but this is not over."

Erica saw the driver pulling up, and she looked at Phil and smiled. "Oh, it's over. You can bet your white ass that it's definitely over." With that being said, she didn't even wait for the driver to come and open her door. She opened the door and instructed her confused driver to take her home.

Erica walked into their home and knew she had to act quickly. She changed and fed Faith and called her parents. She was so angry and hurt at the same time, but she didn't have time to sit and feel sorry for herself. She gathered a few things for her and the baby, and her father assured her that once she got to the airport, a ticket would be waiting for them. She took a cab to the airport instead of using their driver. She breathed a sigh of relief once the plane took off. She was going home, and she would not be returning.

Now that she was back home, Phil had been calling her constantly, making threats about her taking their daughter away. She had already contacted an attorney about handling the divorce and visitation for Faith. She wanted no support from Phil. The only thing she wanted from him was a divorce. Her attorney advised her that he was entitled to visitation and that Phil was actually trying to get custody of their baby. Her father was furious, and he assured her that he would never allow that to happen. Even though Phil had money, so did her parents, and he would not just get his way because of his money.

Erica had to break down and tell her parents and her attorney about what she had endured during the marriage and when she caught him cheating. She almost felt as if the maid knew what was going on and sent her to that room on purpose. She wished there was a way to contact her to find out if this was true and if she was willing to provide a statement to help her case. Her attorney said it would be difficult to get to her, and if they did, she might not be willing to risk her job doing so. Erica was just glad that she was home safe. She just had to keep praying that everything would work out in her favor.

She walked into her bathroom to take a shower. She was excited to see her bestie. They had so much catching up to do.

# CHAPTER 12

Tessa sat in the wheelchair to be taken to see her baby. She felt like her heart was in a million pieces, and she couldn't stop the tears from falling. Her whole body ached, and she felt like she didn't want to live anymore. She looked up at Sam who was standing beside her, and reached up and grabbed his hand. He looked so lost, and she couldn't help him because she was hurting herself.

Tessa had spoken with the detectives and confirmed that David was the one who did this to her. They had been waiting for her to wake up to verify that fact. They had already put out a search for him, but now they were able to get a warrant for his arrest for the attempted murder on her life, and the murder of her baby.

She kept going over the events of that day, trying to figure out what she could have done to save her precious baby. She braced herself as the wheelchair began to move down the hallway to the morgue. When they arrived, the morgue technician brought the baby out wrapped in a blanket, and handed him to Tessa, as she requested. Tessa broke down and held her baby close. "Mommy is so sorry, baby. I should have protected you. Please forgive me, my sweet baby. I love you so much." Tessa let out a loud wail and began to cry. "Why, God?! Why did you take my baby? Please, God! Wake him up, please!" She held her baby close and cried. Sam got down on his knees, hugged Tessa and the baby together, and cried with her. She felt Sam's arms around them, and she cried even harder. Their baby should be alive. This was so unfair.

The nurse walked over and told them it was time for them to go back. Tessa and Sam did not let go. They continued to hold on to their baby and cry. The morgue technician came out to assist the nurse. Tessa would not let go of the baby. "Please, I need more time! Please, don't take him away! He needs his Mommy! Sam, don't let them take him away-- that's our baby!"

Sam stood up and rubbed Tessa's arm. "Baby, we have to let him go. Baby, please let him go. He's gone." Tessa let the baby go. Sam bent over and held her as they both cried together. The nurse came back and wheeled Tessa back to her room.

Once they got her back into her bed, Tessa lay quietly, looking straight ahead. Sobbing, Sam sat on the side of her bed, holding her hand. They stayed that way for quite a while. Tessa finally spoke up. "We have to bury our baby, Sam. I don't want him lying in that morgue. Please get with my family and make arrangements to have a service for him."

Sam looked surprised. "Okay, baby, I will get right on it."

Tessa looked at Sam seriously. "Thank you. Please, go do it now. Don't worry about me. I need some time to myself."

Sam looked unsure about leaving her. Tessa looked at him and placed her hand on his with a sad look on her face. "I'll be fine, Sam. I need you to do this for me." Sam reluctantly agreed to leave her. He made her promise to call him if she needed him. When he left, Tessa broke down and cried again. How was she going to live without her baby? The nurse walked back in to check on her. She gave Tessa something to help her relax, and for the pain Tessa said she was having in her back. She had been through a lot, and she needed to rest so she could deal with tomorrow.

# CHAPTER 13

Yvette walked into Erica's parents' house and screamed at the sight of her best friend. Erica ran down the stairs screaming, and the two women embraced. Yvette pulled away and looked at her best friend. She was still as beautiful as she remembered. She missed her so much, and she regretted not keeping in touch with her. "Erica, I missed you so much!" Yvette felt tears coming out of her eyes.

Erica kissed Yvette on the cheek. "I missed you too, Diva. Come see your goddaughter." Erica grabbed Yvette's hand and led her upstairs to her bedroom.

They walked into Erica's large bedroom, and it brought back fond memories to Yvette. They had spent so much time in this room talking, plotting, scheming, and just hanging out. That was before life got complicated. She walked over to the crib and saw the most beautiful baby she had ever laid eyes on. She looked like a living doll.

Yvette reached down and picked up her beautiful goddaughter. She hugged her and spoke softly. "She is beautiful, Erica, and she looks just like you." She held the baby away from her to look into her beautiful blue eyes. "Hey sweetie, I'm your god-mommy. I'm glad you're here because I intend to spoil you rotten." The baby looked at Yvette, smiled, and held up her little hand to touch Yvette's face. Yvette laughed and felt warm all over from holding her precious goddaughter. It made her look forward to holding her own baby.

Erica walked over to the sitting area in her bedroom and invited Yvette to sit. "Diva, come sit down and have some wine. We have a lot of catching up to do." Yvette joined her friend on the couch, clutching the baby close to her. Little Faith made her feel relaxed and at ease.

Erica spoke up first, "We haven't talked in a long time, and I forgive you, Diva. After my mom told me what had been going on with you, I totally understood. I have some things going on as well, but I'm going to let you go first. You look like you need to vent." Erica poured some wine into the glass, took the baby from Yvette, and placed her on a blanket on the floor with her toys. She poured some wine for herself and sat across from her friend, waiting for her to speak.

Yvette picked up the glass of wine, debating whether she should drink it. She took a sip, and it felt good going down. She also grabbed some wings off the platter that was on the table as well, took off her shoes, and got comfortable. She took another sip of wine and began to tell her side of the story from the beginning. When she mentioned being pregnant, Erica reached over and took her wine glass out of her hand. Yvette protested. "Erica, I really need a drink right now. One glass of wine won't hurt me."

Erica frowned and sighed. Her friend had really gotten herself in some deep shit. She handed the glass back to her, saying, "Finish this one glass, and that's it, Diva. You don't want it to affect your baby. What's your next move? I know you don't want Charles to find out the baby's not his, but you know these things always have a way of coming out, Vette."

Yvette sighed and shook her head as she spoke, "David can't take care of the baby, and he is very dangerous. I'm afraid of what he will try to do to me if he finds out I'm having his baby. I have no money, and my time is limited living with my parents. My only solution is to have Charles take care of us. Hopefully, I can come up with enough money to make David disappear for good."

Erica looked at Yvette with a skeptical look on her face and poured herself another glass of wine. Yvette's issues were deeper than she could have imagined. She didn't know how her friend was going to get out of this mess. She sat back and spoke as gently as she could to her friend. "Diva, you have a lot of different issues going on here. The worst one is your tie to David and murdering your half-sister's baby. I know you didn't tell him to do it, but by the time he's finished trying to save his own ass, it's going to look like you did, sis. You have to figure out a way to break any ties with him, or you're going to spend the rest of your life at his mercy."

Yvette looked at baby Faith playing with her toys. It made her wonder what her baby would be like. She looked at Erica and whispered, "I know. That's what I'm afraid of, Erica. How the hell did I get in so deep? I just wanted to pay them back for what they did to me. Mainly Charles."

Erica shook her head. She should have been here for her friend instead of in Dubai. She could have talked her out of some of these crazy decisions she had made. She made a decision and spoke. "Diva, I will ride with you to Richmond tonight to meet him so you can give him the money. You don't need to go by yourself. There's no telling what he has in mind for you. He may feel that you're just as much of a liability as you feel like he is."

Yvette immediately protested, "No, I won't put you in that type of danger. You have Faith, and I would never forgive myself. I'm going to forward the text to you that he sent me with the address, and if I don't come back, you know where I went and with whom. I need you to do that for me, Erica. I don't even want him to know who you are. I will be fine."

Erica wasn't convinced. "Let me follow you in my car, and if you don't come out by a certain time, I can call the police. I really don't think you should go alone. Not all the way to Richmond!"

Yvette let out a little laugh. "Girl, I already told you about how many times I've been to Richmond and what I've been up to."

"That's the least of my worries. I will be fine, sis. Don't worry. Just keep that address handy, just in case. I don't think he will do anything because, right now, I'm his only cash resource. This cash will get him far away from here, I hope, and maybe he can disappear." Erica thought about what she had just heard from her best friend, and it made her shudder. How did Yvette get herself into all of this? Did she really let greed, jealousy, and anger take over her common sense? Yvette had always been a spoiled brat and stuck up, but so was she to some degree; that's what made them besties. But she would never go this far to get her way. Nevertheless, she was her best friend, and she was going to do what she could to help her and not judge her.

Erica moved over close to her friend and gave her a hug. "I'm here for you, Diva. I just want you to be very careful. What time do you have to go and meet him?"

Yvette looked at her watch. "I have to meet him at midnight."

Erica looked at her watch. "Okay, I want you to text me when you get there and call me when you're on your way back. As a matter of fact, I will stay on the phone with you while you drive there and on your drive back. Don't worry, Diva. I'm back, and we're going to figure this thing out."

Yvette gave her best friend a hug. She loved her so much. She whispered in her ear. "Thanks, Erica. I missed you so much. I know it sounds selfish, but I don't want you to go back."

Erica thought for a minute. "I think you may get your wish, sis."

Yvette let go of Erica and looked at her curiously. "What do you mean by that?"

Erica smiled. "It's a long story. I will tell you about it once you are back from meeting this dude, and you're safe." Yvette nodded and sighed. She agreed. They needed to concentrate on one thing at a time. She really was glad Erica was back.

# CHAPTER 14

Sam pulled up in front of Rome's house in Richmond. He had just left Tessa's parents' house after making funeral arrangements for the baby. He felt tired, sad, and drained. He wanted to go back up to the hospital to be with Tessa, but she told everyone she needed time alone. He figured this was her way of mourning.

Sam had already spoken with the detective to see if there were any leads on locating David, but there were none. They warned him not to try to take the law into his own hands because that would make the situation worse, and it could possibly land him in jail.

He walked up to Rome's door and rang the bell. Rome opened the door, smiled at his friend, and let him in. His arm was in a sling, but other than that, he was doing fine. Sam walked into his friend's house and walked straight to his bar. He poured himself some Hennessy into a glass and downed it in one gulp.

Rome walked up to his friend and put his hand on his shoulder. "Take it easy, man. I know you're going through a lot, but you have to be in your right mind for Tessa."

Sam poured himself another drink and sat down on Rome's couch. "I know, man, but I just can't seem to wrap my mind around all of this. One day everything seemed to be going great, and the next minute my son is dead, my woman and my best friend have been shot, and Yvette is pregnant with my baby."

Rome sat down beside his friend in shock. "WHAT?! How the fuck did that happen, man!?"

Sam shook his head and took a sip of his drink, "That's why I asked you to pick up Tessa that day, man. Yvette showed up at the house with a pregnancy test, saying she was pregnant with my baby. I told you about all the wild and crazy sex we had been having once she busted me. I guess that was all a part of her plan."

Rome was speechless. He took a sip of his drink and sat back. "Sam, man, this is a lot. I wish there was something I could do. How are you going to tell Tessa? Are you sure she's pregnant? You know how conniving she can be."

Sam nodded his head and answered, "I know. That's why I'm meeting her at the doctor's tomorrow to confirm. I haven't thought about what I'm going to do after that. It's just so much, man. News like that could really send Tessa over the edge. You should see her, man. She is just pitiful, and there's nothing I can do about it. I try to stay strong for her, but I'm hurting, too. I lost my son before he even got a chance to take a breath in this world, man. That motherfucker took all of that away from us, and why?"

Rome shook his head. He really hated seeing his friend like this. There wasn't much he could say to make things better; only time and prayer would do that. "Man, you know this too shall pass. It will get easier, and things will fall into place. You may never understand why all of this is happening, but you will get through this. You know I'm here for you. Do you want me to ride with you to go meet Yvette at the doctor's office?"

Sam looked at his friend and smiled. "Yeah, thanks, man, and if you feel up to it, can you go and handle things at the office and on the work sites? I haven't been checking in like I should."

Rome smiled at his friend and nodded. "You got it, man. Let me know if you need anything else. Are the funeral arrangements taken care of?"

Sam sighed. "Angie is handling all of that. I just couldn't do it. She's going to call me tomorrow once everything has been taken care of."

Rome stood up and grabbed Sam's glass to pour him another drink. "Why don't you go and crash in my guest room tonight, man? I know you don't want to be alone."

Sam took the glass and stood up without speaking, walking towards his friend's guest room and closing the door behind him.

# CHAPTER 15

Yvette pulled up to the motel in Richmond. She looked around and waited for David to call her back, as he instructed her to do. About 15 minutes later, he called her and told her to meet him at the 7-Eleven down the block from the motel. Once she arrived, she parked and waited for him to call her back. After making her wait about another 10 minutes, he knocked on her window, scaring the shit out of her. She rolled down the window, and he instructed her to get out of the car and lock her purse and cell phone in the trunk of her car. He grabbed the duffle bag from her. She was reluctant to do so, but she didn't know what else to do at this point.

He stood by, waiting for her to do as she was told. He snatched her keys out of her hands and led her to a large black car with tinted windows. It almost looked like an old police car. He opened the back door and motioned for her to get in. He got in the driver's side and pulled off. They rode for about 20 minutes in silence. He finally spoke, "We need to go over some plans because I need to leave Richmond until things cool down. I need to make sure we're on the same page. I don't want to have to come back to find you or take you down with me. Ya feel me, Ma?" Yvette nodded her head. She was trying to memorize the blocks they were turning on. She had no idea what he was planning to do with her.

David looked over at her and laughed, "Why you looking all scared and shit? I'm not gonna hurt you. We need each other right now. We just need some privacy to go over a plan."

Yvette tried to smile at him to reassure him that she wasn't scared. "I'm not scared, David, and I agree; we need a plan. With the money in that bag, that should hold you for a while and help you to stay under the radar."

David nodded. "Yeah, for a minute. I need to get out of Virginia and try to set me up something to get some cash coming in. I'm going to still need you to keep the cash coming, just in case. And don't get no ideas about changing your number or disappearing because I will always know how to find you. What did you find out about Tessa? Is she talking yet?"

Yvette took a deep breath and answered. "My parents said she spoke to the detectives and named you. They put out a warrant for your arrest. It was on the 11:00 news, but I didn't see it. I was out at my friend's house."

David hit the steering wheel. "SHIT! I NEED TO MAKE SOME MOVES FAST!" Yvette jumped at the sound-- her nerves were shot. David got quiet for a few minutes, and they pulled up to what looked like an abandoned building. He turned off the lights, and it was pitch black. She couldn't even see her hand in front of her face. She was scared to get out of the car. David opened his door and looked over at her, and barked, "What the fuck you waiting for? Get the fuck out!"

Yvette slowly opened the door and got out of the car and waited for him. He grabbed her arm and led her into the dilapidated house. Once inside, he turned on a flashlight and lit a few candles. From what she could see, there were a lot of boxes, a mattress on the floor, and a few empty beer and liquor bottles. It was clear that no one had lived there for years.

David pulled out a bottle of Hennessy and sat on the mattress and motioned for her to sit next to him. He took a long gulp of the Hennessy and passed it to Yvette. She held up her hand in refusal. David shrugged his shoulders, put the bottle on the floor, pulled out a blunt, and lit it. He took a pull and passed it to Yvette, and she took it. She figured she better not refuse him anymore, or else he would become suspicious of her. She took a pull of the blunt and blew it back out, trying not to inhale.

All of a sudden, David was on top of her, ripping off her clothes. She struggled to get him off of her, but he was too strong. David was breathing heavily and kissing her all over her face. She tried to speak in between the struggle. "David, do you think this is a good idea? Don't you think you need to get going while it's still dark?" David stopped and looked down at her, and got off her. He picked up the blunt and took another pull. "Take off your clothes. I have to wait for my man to come through before I leave. So, let's kill some time. We may not see each other for a while."

Yvette wanted to cry. She looked around the run-down house and couldn't imagine what could be crawling around on this dirty mattress. She undressed and stood in front of David. He pulled her down on the mattress and got on top of her. She realized that he was also naked. She didn't even see him undress. He bit her on her neck and all over her breast. He reached between her legs and shoved two of his fingers inside of her. She screamed out in pain. It was like he was in a trance. He worked his fingers in and out of her, and she felt herself getting wet. She couldn't believe her body was reacting to what he was doing to her.

She felt herself about to come, and she screamed. He pulled his fingers out of her wetness and shoved his dick inside of her. He pumped hard, and she screamed some more. She was worried about her baby-- it hurt so badly. He pulled out of her and grabbed her by her hair, and pulled her to her knees. He shoved his dick in her mouth. He grunted, "Open wide and keep it open." He shoved his dick in her mouth, and she began to gag. He kept doing it. He held her by the back of her head. She threw up all over him. She could not control herself. David jumped back and slapped her so hard she went flying off the dirty mattress. He walked over to her and kicked her in the side. "What the fuck is wrong with you!"

Yvette balled up in a fetal position; she did not want her baby to get hurt. She knew she had to do something to calm him down. She looked up. "I'm sorry, David, my stomach has been a little upset with everything going on. Let me make it up to you."

David walked over into the darkness and came back with a rag. He threw it at her, and she wiped up the mess the best way she could. She crawled over to him and wiped him off as well. When he was satisfied that she had cleaned enough, he pushed her down on her knees again. "Assume the position."

Yvette wanted to cry. She turned around and braced herself. He shoved his dick inside her and proceeded to pump her hard from the back. Yvette tried to take it, but she could not bear the pain. "David, you're hurting me! Please, not so hard! Please!!"

This only made David pump harder. The pain was excruciating. David was having the time of his life. "Damn, this pussy is good tonight. Shit, Ma."

Yvette couldn't take it any longer. "Please, David!! Please, I'm pregnant!"

David stopped in mid-stroke. He grabbed her by her hair and said between clenched teeth. "What the fuck did you just say?"

Yvette began to shake and whispered, "I'm pregnant, David."

David let her go and rolled over on the mattress. "What the fuck do you mean you pregnant? Bitch, you don't know how to take no birth control? All that money your peoples spent on you to go to school, and yo ass don't have sense enough to protect yourself?!"

Yvette's body began to shake all over. She felt around for her clothes to cover up. "So much was going on, and I was protecting myself with Charles, but those first few times with you, I didn't expect for us to-- well, you know, and I guess that's when it happened. I just want you to know that this doesn't change anything. You have to leave here, or else we will both be locked up and--"

David stood up and started pacing. "Bitch, you ain't gotta tell me that this don't change nothing! You motherfucking right I have to get out of here, but I ain't no deadbeat. I don't want my seed being born in nobody's prison. Shit! What the fuck else is gonna go wrong?"

Yvette began to get dressed; she didn't know what else to say. David sat back down beside her and looked at her with this weird smile on his face. "Did you tell your folks or anyone?"

Yvette shook her head. "No, I actually go to the doctor tomorrow to confirm the pregnancy. I took a home test, and it was positive. I was getting sick, and I missed my period. I thought it was just stress." She left out that she told Charles that the baby was his or that she told Erica.

David smiled again. "Good. As far as your family and that square-ass nigga is concerned, you only been with him, so he's the daddy. Make that nigga pay us for now."

Yvette let out a sigh of relief. At least she wouldn't have to worry about any trouble from David when it came to the baby.

Now she just needed to form a plan to get Charles to comply, which shouldn't be hard. He had just lost his baby and would not want to lose another blood relative. Yvette felt better and began to get dressed. David watched her get dressed and stood up to take her back to her car. He stopped at the door and turned around and bent down and kissed her deeply. She felt her head spin. This man confused her so much. David looked at her. "When things blow over, I'm coming back to be in my baby's life, Yvette, and I don't want no shit out of you."

Yvette was shocked. "David, how is that going to work? You killed her baby."

David yelled. "You let me worry about that! For now, we will go with the plan, and I will be contacting you when I touch down. Don't fucking play with me, Yvette. Trust me. You will be sorry. If you don't believe me, ask yo sister." He walked out the door and led her back to the car. Once they arrived back at her car, he held her keys out to her. "Don't forget what I told you."

Yvette took her keys and smiled weakly at him. "Don't worry David. We have a plan. I will follow it." Yvette got out of the car and tried to control her urge to run to her car. Once she got in, she drove off. She remembered her purse and phone in the trunk. She got off at the next rest area and took a few deep breaths. She opened the car door and threw up again.

Once she retrieved her purse and phone from the trunk, she saw that Erica had called and texted her over ten times. She prayed she did not call the police. She dialed her number, and she picked up on the first ring. "Yvette, are you okay? I was about to go crazy in here! I didn't know what to do!"

Yvette spoke softly into the phone. "Yes, I'm fine. I guess it could have been worse. I'm on my way back to your house. I really need a hot bath and a warm, comfortable bed to lie in."

Erica was relieved that she was okay. "Girl, I'm so happy to hear your voice. I will stay on the phone with you until you get here, and I will run you a hot bath. Don't worry. We can talk about everything tomorrow. Just get back here in one piece. Also, I will be going with you to the doctor's tomorrow. You shouldn't have to face Charles alone, no matter what the circumstances are. I'm here for you, girl."

Yvette began to cry. She loved her friend so much; she felt bad for being jealous of her all this time. "Thanks, Erica. I'm really glad you're back." Her words couldn't express how much she meant it.

# CHAPTER 16

Tessa sat up in her bed in excruciating pain. She thanked the nurse as she handed her the pain meds. She had just finished her first round of physical therapy, and it was rough. They offered to start in a few days, but she told them she was fine to start immediately. She needed to get herself put back together quickly so that she could get out of the hospital and mourn in the privacy of her own home.

She was tired of the nurses coming in to disturb her thoughts. She'd only managed to get some alone time by sending Sam off to make funeral arrangements for their son. She just wanted to be alone, but no one seemed to understand it. She felt like her heart had been ripped out of her body, and the pain would not stop.

She also had to show the doctor that the physical therapy was working, otherwise, she couldn't be transported to her son's burial-- going to physical therapy was a part of her plan to go see her precious baby boy sooner.

Just as she thought she was going to take a nap and enjoy the effects of the pain meds, her parents walked in the door. She looked at them curiously. She thought they would still be at the funeral home. Her mom read her expression and kissed her cheek. "Hey, baby, everything has been done. Angie just finalized everything for Friday."

Her father walked over and kissed her other cheek. "How was physical therapy?"

Tessa sighed, knowing she won't be going to sleep soon. "It was kind of rough, but they said that's to be expected. Did Angie and Sam make sure they're going to follow my exact instructions?"

Mrs. Grant put her hand over her daughter's. "Yes, baby, every single detail. Have you heard back from the doctor about you going?"

Tessa shook her head. "The nurse said there is a good possibility he will approve it as long as a nurse goes with me, and I am transported by an ambulance. That will be a cost that I will have to pay out of pocket, but that's no problem."

Mr. Grant shook his head. "Tessa, all of that is already taken care of. We just need him to give you the okay."

Tessa looked over to the window and spoke softly, "They want me to see a psychologist, but I refused. I told them I will be fine. I just want to go home."

Mrs. Grant looked at her oldest child, and her heart was breaking into a million pieces for her. "Baby, it might help to talk to someone; just to get it out."

Tessa shook her head. "I don't want to talk to anyone, Mommy. No one, but God, will be able to tell me why this happened, so that's who I need to talk to. No one else has the answers."

Mr. Grant tried to reason with his daughter, "Sweetie, no one may have the answers, but they may be able to help you cope with all of this to move past it."

Tessa shook her head, and tears began to roll down her cheeks. She looked at her father. "Daddy, I will never get past this. I will never forget this moment in my life for as long as I live. And if the police don't find David, I will take whatever money I have to buy a gun and find him myself. I will never stop looking for him. He will pay for what he did to my baby."

Mr. Grant rubbed his daughter's face and shook his head. "Tessa, I won't say I know how you feel because I never lost a child, but I came pretty damn close to it, and I never want to experience that feeling again. You need to let the police handle this one, baby. They will find him, and he will pay."

Tessa just looked at her father. "And what if they don't find him, Daddy? It will just turn into a cold case, and he will get away with it. He needs to die like my innocent baby died. For the life of me, I don't understand why Sam is not out there looking for him instead of sitting here staring at me all day."

Mr. and Mrs. Grant sat there, stunned at her last statement. They didn't know what to say. She was mourning, and they knew she really needed to talk to someone before she left the hospital.

Mrs. Grant looked at her daughter and spoke carefully. "Tessa, Sam is hurting just as much as you are. He is trying to keep it together to be there for you and deal with his own grief at the same time. He has already been warned by the detectives not to take matters into his own hands. The last thing we need right now is for him to get locked up."

Tessa looked at her mother and mumbled under her breath, "Humph."

Before anyone could say anything else, Angela walked into the room. She walked over, smiled, and gave her sister a hug and kiss. "Hi, Sissy. How was physical therapy today?"

Tessa looked at her sister, ignored her question, and asked. "Have all the arrangements been made for little Sam's funeral?"

Angela was taken aback by her sister's abruptness. She raised her eyebrows and answered, "Um, yeah, everything has been arranged according to your instructions, Sissy."

Tessa had a blank look on her face. "Good."

Angela sat in the chair next to her sister and looked at her strangely. She tried to make conversation with her, so she asked her again. "How was physical therapy, Tessa?"

Tessa looked at her sister with annoyance on her face. "Angie, it was painful, but not as painful as sitting here knowing my baby is downstairs on a cold slab, dead."

Angie sat with her mouth open in shock. She decided to try a different approach. "Sissy, I know this is a difficult time for you, but please know that we are all here for you. Whatever you need, just tell me, Tess."

Tessa sat up and looked directly at her sister. "Angie, you have no idea how difficult this is for me. You get to go home to your babies, kiss them, hold them, and watch them grow up. I don't get that privilege. My baby is dead! Gone, Angie! He's not coming back! His life was over before it even started! So, don't sit there and tell me you know about my difficult time because you have no fucking idea! None of you do!"

Mrs. Grant stood up and looked at Tessa. "You are right, baby, we don't know how you feel, but all we can do is be here for you and try to comfort you. Now I understand you're grieving, so I'm going to give you a pass on your behavior. Your sister is only trying to help you and make things a little easier for you. We can't take away your pain, but we are doing the best we can to try to help you along. We're family, and we are going to be here no matter what. We just want you to get better, Tessa. We don't want you to forget what happened. Hell, none of us will forget, but we have to stick together and be there for one another. "

Tessa nodded her head. "I'm sorry for my outburst."

Angie hugged her sister. "It's okay, Sissy. You're going through a really tough time right now. Why don't you try to get some rest and we can come back later? I'm going to check on the progress of the boutique and take care of a few other things."

Everyone walked over and gave Tessa a kiss. Mrs. Grant stopped before walking out of the door and turned around. "Ed and Maggie wanted to come up and see you today. Should I tell them to come up tomorrow?"

Tessa closed her eyes. "Yeah, tell them tomorrow will be a better day for me. I've had all I can handle for one day." Mrs. Grant nodded and exited the room.

# CHAPTER 17

Yvette and Erica pulled up to the doctor's office. Yvette was a nervous wreck. Erica looked at her friend and smiled. "Girl, look at you. Are you okay? Do you have to throw up again?"

Yvette took some deep breaths and a few sips of water. She'd thrown up three times this morning. She felt so weak and tired. Yvette shook her head. "No, I don't think so. I just want to get this over with Erica."

The women got out of the car and walked into the medical building. While they were waiting for the elevator, Charles and Rome walked up. Yvette sucked her teeth and rolled her eyes at the sight of Rome. The two men walked up, and Charles was the first to speak. "Good morning, ladies. Erica, it's good to see you. When did you get back in town?"

Erica walked over and gave Charles a hug, she knew Yvette wouldn't like it, but it was time for everyone to start acting like adults. There was a baby involved, and someone had to grow up here. She was starting to feel bad about having information on who did this to his precious baby. She looked at Charles and smiled. "Hey, Charles. I've been back about a week now. I heard about what happened. I'm so sorry. I can't imagine how you must feel."

Charles gave Erica a sad smile. "Thanks, Erica, it's been really tough."

Yvette continued to ignore both men until the elevator came. They all stepped in, where Rome looked at Erica and smiled. "Hi, Erica. I think we met once before." He held out his hand.

Erica took his hand and smiled. "Rome, right? We met at the engagement party." As soon as she said it, she regretted it.

Yvette chimed in. "Yeah, what a joke." After that, they all decided to be silent the rest of the way to the doctor's office. Once inside the office, Yvette signed in, and they all sat and waited for Yvette to be called. The nurse walked out and called her; Charles got up and followed her in. Erica went to get up, but Yvette stopped her. "I will be okay, Erica. You can wait out here." Erica nodded, sat back down, and made small talk with Rome.

Once inside the examination room, the nurse gave Yvette a cup for a urine sample. Sam sat in the examination room, waiting patiently. Yvette returned and sat on the examination table. They were both quiet for a few minutes. Yvette finally broke the silence. "Once you get this confirmed, where do we go from here? I have a long road ahead of me, and I don't want to go through this alone. I know this isn't an ideal situation, but it is what it is. The baby will be here in a matter of months, and it deserves to be taken care of and have both parents in its life. You're always talking about being honorable, and I'm expecting you to do the honorable thing. I know you're going through a tragedy right now, but my baby shouldn't have to be neglected because of it."

Charles sat silently and allowed her to talk. He thought for a minute before he spoke. "Yvette, if you're pregnant, I intend to do the right thing by my child. What's done is done."

Yvette became angry and hissed. "*What's done is fucking done?* Is that all you have to say about your unborn child? What, you only have enough love in your cold heart for Tessa and your dead baby? This baby is alive inside of me, Charles, and it's yours! It will not be dismissed or pushed aside. I'm going to make sure of that. When I leave here, I intend to tell my parents. You can come along if you like, but they're finding out today!"

Charles looked at her in disbelief. "Yvette, I'm about to have a funeral service for my son. Your parents' grandson. Can't you at least wait until all of this is over?"

Just as Yvette was about to answer, Dr. Simmons walked in. She looked at Yvette and smiled. She had been her gynecologist ever since Yvette was sixteen. She sat down. "So, I see we're going to have a baby. I'm about to have the nurse come in and prep you for a sonogram, just to be sure and to find out how far along you are."

Yvette looked at Charles and smiled. She was so happy. She couldn't read the look on his face, and she didn't care. All she knew was that she was about to have a baby, and her life was going to get back on track. She still hadn't figured out what she was going to do about David, but she would just have to cross that bridge when she got to it. She rubbed her stomach and spoke to Charles. "To answer your question-- no, I will not wait. This is happy news for me, and I plan to share it. I have nothing to be ashamed of. You do."

Charles sat, silently staring at the floor. He didn't say a word. Yvette wasn't worried about his silence. In time, he would come around. This baby would take the place of the one he lost. The nurse walked in and prepped her for the sonogram. She was excited. The doctor returned, and as she performed the sonogram, the room filled with the sound of the baby's heartbeat. Yvette began to laugh. Charles continued to sit silently. When it was over, they walked out into the waiting room together.

Yvette took note of how Rome and Erica seemed so chummy, laughing and talking. Erica rushed over to Yvette, all smiles, holding the sonogram pictures. "Erica, I heard my baby's heartbeat, and I'm due in seven months!"

Erica gave her friend a hug. "I'm so happy for you, Yvette! Congratulations!"

Rome and Charles stood by quietly. Yvette turned around and looked at Charles. "So, I'm off to tell my parents. Are you going to join me?"

Charles nodded his head. "I'll meet you over there." He walked off and headed out of the building to his car.

Erica walked out with her friend, holding her hand. "Diva, are you sure now is the right time to tell them with everything going on?"

Yvette looked at her friend like she was crazy. "Of course! This will be their first grandchild-- in reality. They will be happy for me. They know I've been through a lot, and they should be happy to see me happy. Erica, I'm not going to downplay the joy I feel for the new life I'm bringing into the world. It's not fair." Erica didn't say anything. She just got into the car with her friend and prayed things would go well. She had a bad feeling about all of this. She promised to be there for her, and she was going to keep her promise.

# CHAPTER 18

Rome drove his friend over to the Duncan's house. He looked over at Sam and shook his head-- he really felt for his best friend and brother. He turned down the radio and tried to get him to talk. "Man, do you think this is a good idea, telling them so soon about the baby?"

Sam looked out of the window. "It's not my idea, man. It's Yvette's. I agreed to be there so she won't tell any lies on me."

Rome muttered, "Damn."

Sam shook his head. "That's what I said. I'm having a funeral service for my son on Friday. I'm on my way to tell my ex-fiancé's parents that I knocked up their other daughter. Tessa's in the hospital acting like she don't want me around. I feel like I'm going crazy, man."

"I'm trying hard to keep it together, and I can't help but wonder if Yvette trapped me on purpose. She was always so diligent about using protection. I just don't get it.'"

Rome shook his head. "To be honest, something just don't seem right about this, man. Yvette is plain evil, and I don't put anything past her. If you have to deal with her for the next 18 years, I hate to think what your life is going to be like. And, man, when and how are you going to tell Tessa?"

Sam continued to look out the window. He began to rub his temples-- he was beginning to get another headache. He didn't want to talk about it anymore. He looked over at Rome as if he was seeing him for the first time. "Man, how the hell are you driving with your arm in a sling?"

Rome laughed. "Look, you're in no shape to be driving. I got this. You're in good hands. I drive very well with my right hand." Sam laughed. It was the first time he laughed in days. Rome was truly a good friend to him.

He wanted to get off the subject of his miserable life, so he decided to get into Rome's business. "I noticed how you and Erica were hitting it off in the doctor's office."

Rome laughed. "Don't be trying to start nothing, man. We were just talking, but she is sexy."

Sam laughed. "Yeah, she is. She's also married with a baby."

Rome rolled his eyes. "Yeah, to some old white guy that's in Dubai. He ain't hittin' it right."

Sam looked at him, surprised. "How do you know? She told you?"

Rome laughed. "I can tell when a woman is not getting the dick like they should, and she's definitely not getting the dick. If she was, she wouldn't have left him in Dubai."

Sam laughed. "Okay, man, if you say so."

Rome pulled up in front of the Duncan's mansion. "On the serious side, she seems to be really cool and down to earth. She's nothing like her friend. If she wasn't married, I would make a play for her."

Sam sighed. "Well, you might have a chance if what you think about her is true. What is she doing here, and her husband is in Dubai?"

Rome smiled. "Good question. I might just ask her the next time I talk to her. When you guys were back with the doctor, we decided that we can be the mediators between you two if that would make things easier. She said she would talk to Yvette about it, and I told her I would speak with you."

Sam looked surprised. "What else did y'all discuss?"

Rome said. "Oh, this and that. I told you, she's real cool. Easy to talk to."

Sam opened the car door. "Well, after this conversation, I'm sure we will need some mediation." Rome sat in the car as Sam got out.

Sam looked back. "What are you just sitting there for? Bring your ass on in here with me, man."

Rome laughed and got out of the car to follow his friend.

# CHAPTER 19

Tessa sat in her room and stared at the television. She wasn't really watching it until David's face popped up on the screen. The reporter went into detail about how he was wanted on two counts of attempted murder, attempted kidnapping, and the murder of an unborn fetus. She went on about how she and Rome were gunned down in front of her house and how he was her ex-boyfriend that she had put away for domestic abuse. She said his motive wasn't clear. They didn't know why he attempted to kidnap her or why he shot her and Rome. He was considered armed and dangerous, and anyone who saw him should not approach him but call the authorities.

Tessa stared at the screen. It made her angry to see David's face. She looked at the clock and wondered where Sam could be. She wasn't really worried because she was fine being alone.

The doctor came in and told her that they were going to make arrangements for her to go to the funeral for her baby. That made her happy.

Her main concern was getting out of the hospital and hiring a PI to find David-- he needed to die. She didn't care about going to jail. As far as she was concerned, her life ended when her baby's life ended.

She picked up her phone and texted Sam. She also pressed the button on her IV to get another dose of her pain meds.

Sam texted her back and told her he was tying up some loose ends at the office and that he would be there with her food as soon as he finished. He ended the text by telling her he loved her. She didn't respond. She didn't want to feel anything anymore.

# CHAPTER 20

Yvette walked into her parents' den with Erica following behind her. Her parents were on the couch watching television, relaxing. They had planned to go to the hospital to sit with Tessa, but Elizabeth called and told them she had a rough day and that tomorrow would be better. Maggie looked up, saw the girls, and smiled. "Well, Frick and Frack are back together again."

Erica walked in and gave Maggie a hug and kiss. "Hello, Ms. Maggie. It's so good to see you."

Maggie hugged her back. "Hi Erica, you look great! You can't even tell you had a baby! Married life and motherhood are definitely agreeing with you! Isn't it, Ed?"

Ed stood up and gave Erica a hug. He looked sad and tired, but he smiled. "Yes, Erica, you are glowing. How's Phil?"

Erica sat down. "He's fine. By the way, I'm so sorry about what happened."

Ed smiled. "So am I, darling. You just never know what can happen. That is why you have to be good to people while you have the chance."

The doorbell rang, and Charles and Rome entered the den. Ed stood up, looking surprised. "Charlie! Come in, son. How are you holding up?"

He walked over to Ed and gave him a hug. "I'm hanging in there. Taking one day at a time."

Maggie stood up and gave him a hug. "How is Tessa today?"

He hugged her back. "She just texted me asking for food, so I'm taking that as a sign of improvement."

Ed looked at Rome and gave him a hug. "How are you holding up, Rome? Do you need anything? I can't thank you enough for showing up when you did and stopping that fool from taking Tessa. I know it still turned out bad, but I feel it would have been worse if he had gotten her in that van. I'm just sorry that anyone got hurt."

Rome nodded, "I'm good, sir, and I'm glad I got there in time to stop him. I just wish I could have stopped everything altogether."

Maggie walked over to Rome and gave him a hug, "Everything happens for a reason, baby. Just let us know if you need anything."

Rome smiled. "Thanks, ma'am."

Yvette finally spoke up. "Mommy and Daddy, we're all here because I have some good news. I think this family could use some good news after all of this."

Maggie and Ed sat down, looked at their daughter, and smiled. Maggie spoke to her daughter. "Well, Vette, tell us your good news. Lord knows we can use it."

Yvette stood up, smiled, and began to speak to her audience. "What I'm about to tell you guys may not seem ideal at the time, but, nevertheless, it's still good news. The circumstance may not be ideal, but it is what it is. Mommy and Daddy, me and Charles are having a baby!"

The room was silent. Yvette looked at her parents, who sat looking at her like she had three heads. Maggie was the first to speak. "Lil girl, what the hell did you just say?"

Yvette backed up from her mother and said it again softly. "I'm pregnant, Mommy-- your baby is having a baby."

Maggie jumped up, and her husband stopped her. "Maggie, baby, please don't. There's been too much hurt and pain in this family already. Let's try to be calm and think this thing through. Yvette is right about one thing-- the circumstances aren't ideal, but there is another grandchild on the way."

Maggie snatched away from her husband. "Rome and Erica, can you all excuse us? Go down out on the patio, and I will have some snacks and drinks sent out to you guys."

After the pair left the room, Maggie called Ethel to make them some refreshments. She sat down and looked from Charles to Yvette, but she didn't say anything. This made Yvette nervous. Ed spoke first. "Okay, somebody talk to me and tell me the truth because I'm in no mood for any more bullshit from you or Charlie. Charlie, you talk. We have heard enough from Vette for the moment."

Charles cleared his throat. He didn't know what to say, but he tried, "Well, sir, Yvette met me at the house the day Tessa was shot and told me she was pregnant. I went over to the house because a neighbor called about the sprinkler. It was malfunctioning, and I had to go and dismantle the wires because the yard was flooded. Yvette walked in when I was walking out and gave me the news."

Maggie glared at her daughter. "Vette, how did you know where to find Charlie? We told you we would all be at the shower."

Yvette felt herself begin to sweat. "The neighbor also called me because he couldn't get through to Charles."

Maggie stared at her daughter. "But Charlie just said he did talk to the neighbor. Isn't that what you said, Charlie?"

Charles felt himself sweating as well. "Well, actually, my assistant gave me the message."

Maggie's eyes narrowed as she looked at her daughter, "Continue, Charlie."

He cleared his throat again and continued. "She showed me a positive pregnancy test and said she was pregnant and she was keeping the baby. I told her that

I wanted to go with her to her doctor's appointment to confirm, and we would go from there."

Maggie sat quietly, looking at her daughter. This made Yvette extremely uncomfortable. Ed spoke up. "So, I guess even though everything else was going wrong in the relationship, things in the bedroom were just fine, and no one tried to be responsible."

Charles spoke up. "Sir, not trying to be disrespectful, but your daughter always made sure she was protected. She told me on many occasions that she didn't want a baby until we were married at least five years, and she didn't want to ruin her body at such a young age. She always made sure she was, well, you know before anything happened with us. I was just as shocked as you are now. But I plan to take care of my responsibilities. I will be meeting with my lawyer to put something in place financially for the baby, and hopefully, we can get our attorneys together to come up with an amicable co-parenting agreement."

Ed shook his head. "And what about Tessa?"

Charles put his head in his hands. "I have to figure out when and how to tell her. This is all too much. Please believe me when I say I didn't intend for this to happen, and I plan to take full responsibility for all of it, sir. I just need to figure things out."

Ed stood up. "Charlie, this is the biggest mess I have ever encountered in my life, and I just don't know what to think at this moment. I do know that innocent lives are being affected by all of this, and y'all need to figure this out. This news might be the thing that sends

Tessa over the edge, but we also have to think about Vette and the baby. I don't think any decisions need to be made right now because we're all too emotional. Let's get through this funeral and get Tessa out of that hospital, and then we will deal with this issue. Right now, I can't even think straight." Ed got up and walked out of the den. He was done for the day.

Maggie sat looking at her daughter. "Charles, why don't you head over to the hospital and take Tessa some food? I need to talk to my daughter alone."

She didn't have to tell him twice. He jumped up, saying, "Yes, ma'am." He walked out of the den, leaving Yvette to deal with her mother.

Yvette sat very still, waiting for her mother to speak. Maggie sat staring at her daughter for a minute before she finally spoke. "You know, you can fool your Daddy and your friends and Charles, but I gave birth to your ass, and you will never fool me, Vette, at least not for long. Now Charlie is too distraught to think about how the hell you ended up at that house the same time he did. And what? You travel with a pregnancy test in your pocketbook? You told me out of your own mouth that you weren't having any babies any time soon. Now, all of a sudden, you're happily pregnant by a man who is in love with another woman."

"Not to mention, that woman is your sister who just lost her baby in the most tragic way. I sat here and stared at you, Vette, to see if I could see your soul. I sat here looking at you to figure out what the hell was going on in your brain. I knew something was going on.

Things were just too damn quiet around here. But I gave you the benefit of the doubt. I said, maybe she is just trying to come to terms with things. Now that girl is lying up in that hospital, and her baby is dead, and all of a sudden, you come up pregnant by Charles. Something ain't right, and something stinks. And where there is stink, there is some shit somewhere. And I'm gonna find it, Vette. Mark my words."

Yvette started to cry. "Mommy, I thought you would be happy that I am having your grandbaby. Why is everything about Tessa? What about me and my feelings? What about your grandchild?"

Maggie stood up and walked towards the door. "Vette, when you are ready to come to me with the truth, you will know where to find me." Maggie walked out of the den and went to be with her husband. Yvette sat on the couch alone and cried. This wasn't turning out at all how she had planned. She knew one thing-- she needed to steer clear of her mother. She meant what she said when she said she would get to the bottom of things, and that scared her even more than David and going to jail.

# CHAPTER 21

Tessa sat in the funeral home in front of the tiny white casket. She leaned over and looked down at her beautiful son. He was dressed in a white christening outfit-- per her request.

He looked so peaceful. She kissed his fingers and reached over and touched his little face. She spoke softly, "I love you, Charles Samuel Thompson Jr. Sleep in peace, my little angel."

She felt Sam place his hand on her shoulder. She reached up and grabbed his hand and kissed it. Their baby was really gone, and there was nothing they could do to bring him back to them. She felt Sam trembling, and she squeezed his hand tighter. She felt bad for the way she had been treating him. Little Sam was his only blood relative, and he was about to bury him just like his other ones.

She vowed to pay David back for doing this to their family. She worked hard with her physical therapist to try and get the strength back in her legs. She had even started talking to the psychologist, saying what she knew they wanted to hear to get her out of there. She had asked Angie to bring her laptop so she could start checking on her business and researching private detectives. She needed a PI to assist her in locating David before the cops got him.

Sam's voice interrupted her thoughts. "Baby, it's time."

Tessa nodded. She knew what he meant. They were about to close the casket. The service was over, and everyone had viewed the baby and paid their respects.

She allowed Sam to roll her wheelchair back to where her family was seated. She looked at her parents: Elizabeth, George, Ed, and Maggie. They were so distraught. She gave them a sad smile. She looked over at Angie. She was quietly crying. Then someone caught her eye. At first, she didn't recognize the person until they made eye contact. It was Yvette. She was sitting with a very attractive woman she didn't recognize. Yvette had a strange look on her face, but Tessa couldn't read the look. She quickly looked away.

After they closed the casket, everyone was dismissed. Tessa had to go back to the hospital, so there wasn't a repass after the service, and she was glad. Her back was starting to hurt, and she needed her pain meds. The baby was being cremated, and now they would have to try to go on with their lives. Sam pushed her through the crowd, occasionally stopping for someone to give her a hug or words of encouragement. It was taking all the strength she had not to scream for everyone to get out of her way and leave her alone.

Once she was back in the ambulance alone with Sam and the nurse, Tessa felt at ease. She was actually glad to get back to the hospital, away from it all.

Sam was quiet and sad. She reached out and held his hand. He took her hand and brought it to his lips. She looked at Sam. "How are you holding up, sweetie?"

Sam looked at her, shaking his head. "I still can't believe he's gone, Tess. I'm trying to cope, but it's hard. He was our baby. Our son."

Tessa looked at the man she loved and sighed. She touched his leg. "Don't worry, sweetie. We have each other. We will somehow make it through."

She paused a moment before asking him her question. "Did you know Yvette was going to be there? Did Ed and Maggie make her come?"

Sam stiffened and looked away. "I'm not sure. I was surprised to see her there myself."

Tessa shook her head and closed her eyes. She couldn't wait to get back to the hospital to get some rest and her meds.

After a month of intense counseling and physical therapy, the doctor told Tessa with her progress, there was a good chance that she might be able to go home within the week-- she would just go to outpatient therapy.

Tessa was glad to hear that. She really had a lot to do. When she arrived at her room, the nurse and Sam settled her down in her bed to relax, and she was able to get some medication. Just as they finished, both sets of her parents, and Angie, came through the door with food. Angie had her laptop. She was actually glad to see them.

They all sat around Tessa, and she was grateful for their love and support. Little Sam would have gotten so much love from her family.

Ed looked at Tessa. "You really look good, Tessa. I hear the doctor may release you next week."

Tessa smiled. "Yes, that's great news. The best news I've gotten in a while. I still have a long road to recovery, but I'm getting there, I guess."

Sam sat on the side of her bed and put his arm around her. She rested her head on his shoulder. She couldn't wait to go home and just sleep in the comfort of his arms all night. She missed him so much, and she needed him right now.

Her family stayed about an hour before saying their goodbyes and leaving Tessa and Sam alone. Sam hadn't left her side since the funeral, and she was glad. He got up and sat in the chair next to her bed. "If it's okay, I'm going to stay here with you tonight. I just don't want to be alone. I don't want to leave you, Tessa."

She smiled at him and held her arms out. "Why are you all the way over there? Come and lay with me and hold me, please." Sam got up and joined her again on the bed. He put his arms around her, and they both fell asleep.

# CHAPTER 22

When the family got outside, Ed stopped to talk to the Grants. "Look, a situation has come up that I think we need to make you all aware of. I think we should all go somewhere and have a talk."

Angie answered for everyone. "We can all go back to my place. It's about 15 minutes from here, and we can have some privacy. You can follow me." The group went to their cars and headed to Angie's house. When they arrived, her girls were in the backyard playing. They did not attend the services. It was decided that it would be too much for them to see their baby cousin lying in a casket. Since her husband was a truck driver and was out of town working, he could not take off for the services. So, Angie had the girls stay home with a sitter. Angie thanked and paid the sitter, then went out to check on the girls.

Elizabeth led the Duncans to Angie's den and told them to make themselves comfortable. She offered them some refreshments, but they refused. They really wanted to get this conversation over with.

Angie returned and joined everyone in the den. Ed stood up and began pacing and started talking. "I don't know where to begin. So much has happened these last few months, and it just keeps getting worse. I guess there is no other way to do this but to get to the point. Yvette is pregnant with Charles' baby."

Elizabeth yelled. "Oh, my God! My poor Tessa!" Angie sat there, shocked into silence, and so was George.

Ed continued. "I had the same reaction, and so did Maggie-- to a point. We felt we needed to give you all a heads-up and figure out how to handle all of this. I don't have to explain to you all what type of person Yvette is, but she is having my grandchild, and Charles is the father. I'm not defending her-- I just need to make sure that this is handled properly. Tessa is very delicate, and I don't want to bring her any more pain or sorrow. I'm at a loss for words. I just don't know what to do or how to feel." Ed sat down and held his head in his hands. He felt so tired and weary.

Maggie rubbed her husband's back and spoke. "I am so sorry about this, and I want you to know that I have spoken to my daughter to let her know that I am aware of the fact that something's not right, and I will get to the bottom of whatever is going on."

Elizabeth broke down and cried, and George tried to comfort her. Angela finally found her voice. "Does Sam know about the baby?"

Maggie nodded her head and answered. "Yes, he came along with Yvette to inform us yesterday. For the record, he is not overjoyed about this situation. He let us know that he has every intention of taking care of his responsibilities, but I'm sure my daughter has another agenda, and that's my concern."

Angela frowned. "That is also my concern, along with my sister's welfare. How and when did all of this happen?"

Maggie shook her head, thinking about the situation. "According to what we were told, it happened after Yvette confronted them with her findings about them. She and Charles were still engaging and not protecting themselves."

Angie shook her head. She knew exactly what Yvette was up to, and she wanted to kick her narrow ass. Angie frowned again. "Look, Mr. and Mrs. Duncan, I love my sister very much, and I'm not about to sit by and let your daughter hurt her again. This is all just too much, and your daughter needs to be stopped. I mean, what the hell is wrong with this broad?"

George spoke up and chastised Angela, "Watch your language and your tone, Angie. Ed and Maggie had nothing to do with what's going on. And they didn't have to tell us."

Maggie sighed. "No, George, Yvette is our responsibility, and we need to protect Tessa."

George shook his head. "I think we need to have a conversation with Sam to see where his head is. This is just a mess. I don't know how much more Tessa will be able to take before she reaches her breaking point, and with that psycho still out there, she isn't safe."

Elizabeth spoke up. "We need to keep this from Tessa for as long as we can. She needs to recover from the loss of her baby and the trauma of her injury. Please keep your daughter away from her. I will get with Sam tomorrow to discuss things with him. This is just another thing to add to the list of things she will stress about, and it's so unfair to her."

Elizabeth shook her head and started to cry again. Angela went over to her mother to comfort her. "We will call Sam tomorrow and discuss with him how to handle everything. Please try to control your daughter. I'm not sure what I will do to her if I see she is trying to hurt my sister again. I don't care what her condition is."

Elizabeth grabbed Angela's hand. "Angie, don't we have enough hurt in this family already? Please don't talk like that."

Everyone sat quietly, reflecting on the situation and what was to come. No one really had the answers, and no one really understood what was going on and how deep it really was. All they knew was things were not about to get better anytime soon, and they needed to protect Tessa as much as they could.

# CHAPTER 23

Erica lay on her stomach and moaned. She had never experienced the pleasure that she was feeling at the moment. She closed her eyes and enjoyed what Rome was doing to her.

He was kissing her all over her back, down her ass, and all the way down to the heels of her feet. He came back up and lifted her up by her hips so that her ass was sticking up. He spread her cheeks and started licking her pussy from behind. She tensed up and moaned even louder. "Yes, don't stop. It feels so good, baby." Rome stuck his finger in her pussy and worked it in and out until she was dripping wet. He rose up and slid his dick inside of her. She moaned again and started moving her ass to meet his thrust.

Rome grunted and grabbed her by her hips so he could bury his dick deeper inside of her. "Shit, E, this pussy is good." Erica smiled and used her pussy muscles to squeeze his dick each time he entered her, making Rome increase the pace. He began to fuck her faster and harder.

"Yeah, Rome! Fuck me, baby! Don't stop!" Rome fucked her harder, and Erica's body began to shake as she felt spasm after spasm yank through her body. She screamed and pushed her ass back harder. "Shit, Rome, I'm coming again!"

Rome smiled and ground his dick deep in her pussy, and that sent her over the edge. Erica grabbed the sheets and screamed at the top of her lungs. Rome pulled his dick out of her. and she squirted all over the sheets. Rome laughed and collapsed beside her. Erica was still on her stomach and breathing heavily. She looked at him and busted out laughing.

She and Rome had been seeing each other for about a month--they began to talk and text every day after they all went to the doctor's office that day with Yvette. They exchanged information when they agreed to be mediators for Yvette and Sam. Rome ended up calling her that next day, and they had a great conversation and ended up talking for hours. She told him about her marriage, and he told her about his life and how he grew up.

Yvette had painted him to be the worst person in the world, but she was finding out that was nowhere near the truth. He was smart, kind, funny, considerate, and sexy as hell. Rome was tall and muscular. He wore his soft hair cut close and had a goatee. He had swag about him that turned her on. He was close to his mom and took care of her. He was also very loyal to his best friend.

As they talked about the situation between Yvette and Sam, she realized how much growing up her friend had to do. She couldn't reveal the truth about the baby to Rome because she was also loyal to her best friend, but she was really feeling Rome. She could tell that he felt the same, and she knew sooner or later, things would become complicated if Yvette ever found out that they were seeing each other. No one but Sam, knew their secret.

Rome stared at her and started rubbing her back. She closed her eyes and smiled. She loved the way he was so attentive to her. She hadn't brought Faith around him yet because she didn't feel like it was the right time. They had been spending as much time together as they could or whenever she could escape Yvette.

The further along Yvette got into her pregnancy, the more she seemed to depend on her. Along with Yvette, Erica also had to deal with Phil calling and threatening to come to the States and take Faith back to Dubai. He even threatened to contact the authorities to have Faith sent back to Dubai because she wasn't a citizen of the U.S.

He made it clear that he couldn't care less if Erica remained in the U.S., but his daughter belonged with him-- Erica would die before she let her baby go. He was not in any position to take care of a baby, and his parents treated Erica and Faith as if they were still in the days of Jim Crow. They refused to stay in their home when in Dubai and never even called or came to see Faith. Hell, they came to the wedding and left right after the ceremony, stating some bull about his mom not feeling well. She would never give her baby up to that family.

Rome stood up and went into his bathroom. Erica heard the water running in the bathtub. He came back out and pulled her up out of bed. "Come take a bath with me, sexy."

Erica got up out of bed and followed him into the bathroom. He had candles lit and bubbles in the bathwater. She smiled and stepped into the tub. She felt Rome get in behind her, and she leaned back onto his chest and enjoyed the hot water all over her body.

Rome rubbed her shoulders and kissed her on the neck. "You know, E, I never felt like this about a woman. I actually enjoy being with you. Usually, after sex, I'm ready to leave or for the woman to leave, but when we're together, I never want our time together to end. I sit and wonder how the hell you are friends with Yvette. Y'all are nothing alike."

Erica laughed at the truth in his statement. "She actually does have some good traits. She's not all bad-- you really have to get to know Yvette to see the good side of her. I do admit I've seen a change in her since I've been gone, but I guess a lot has happened. She's like a sister to me, and I just want her to be okay."

Rome nodded his head in understanding. "I get that, and that's what attracts me to you the most: your sense of loyalty. You're mad cool and down to earth. If this situation wasn't so fucked up, I would definitely take you to meet Tessa. You guys are so much alike. You would really like her."

Erica smiled. "I'm sure she is a very nice person, from what I have heard from you and piecing together what Yvette has told me. I do recognize that she was actually the real victim in all of this, and my heart truly goes out to her. I pray that things will turn around for the best for all parties involved."

"It's a losing situation for all." Rome kissed her on her neck. "I guess you're right, E."

Erica closed her eyes and enjoyed her time with Rome. She couldn't help but wonder what the future would hold for all of them. Especially for Yvette-- she was so tangled up in her lies and deceit that there was no way that this was going to be a happy ending for her, but she hadn't figured out a way to tell Yvette this without upsetting her. She considered going to the Duncans and telling them everything Yvette told her, but that would definitely end their friendship. She loved Yvette, and she didn't want anything bad to happen to her. If she told anybody, and if something happened to Yvette, she would feel terrible knowing that she didn't do anything to prevent it.

Then, there was this thing she had going on with Rome. She certainly didn't want him to think that she had participated in any of this messiness. She just did not know what to do or who to turn to. She felt stressed out with everything going on with Phil and trying to make sure that Yvette didn't end up in jail or dead. She needed a drink. "Baby, do you have any more wine?"

# CHAPTER 24

Tessa had been home for a month, and she had been progressing just fine, according to the doctors. She was now walking on her own, but she had not gone to counseling. She and Sam had been working side by side trying to get her boutique back up and running.

Physically, she felt better, and she had dropped 80 pounds due to the trauma and stress-- she was still losing weight.

Her office was finished, so she and Sam went in together every day. She did paperwork while he and his crew worked on the renovations. She had been in contact with a PI, and there had not been any leads on David. It was as if he had disappeared off the face of the earth.

Mason, her PI, also told her that someone had to be financing his disappearance. There was no way a guy with no means of income could evade the police for this long.

Sam had no idea that she was searching for David or that she had gone out to apply for a gun permit. Her dad had taught her and Angie how to shoot a gun when they were teenagers because he felt they should know how to defend themselves. She never liked guns, but now she understood what her father meant.

Sam hadn't left her side since she got out of the hospital. He had been so attentive and kind to her. She loved Sam, she truly did, but she felt as if she could not move forward in their relationship until she settled the score with David once and for all. He took something from them that they could never get back, and she wasn't about to let him get away with it.

"Hey, babe, I'm about to take Calvin home to babysit while his mother goes and runs some errands. Do you want to ride with me?"

Tessa shook her head. "Go ahead, sweetie, Angie is on her way, and we're going to the bank and the fabric store to take care of some business. We need to start replenishing for the grand re-opening. We're also going to the mall-- I need to buy some new clothes. I can't wear any of my old clothing. Everything is falling off of me."

Sam walked over and gave her a kiss on her cheek. "Rome is out here working with the guys. Do you want me to send him with you guys?"

Tessa waved him off. "No, sweetie. We will be fine. You can't be with me every moment, Sam."

Sam hugged her really tight. "You are right, baby. Just be careful."

Tessa kissed him on the lips. "I will, sweetie. Go do what you have to do." Tessa reached into her purse and pulled out her pain pills, popping two in her mouth and drowning them with some water.

Angie walked into the office. "Okay, Tessa, we got business to take care of."

Tessa grabbed her purse. "Let's go!" The sisters walked out to Angie's car and headed to the bank. They took care of their business and headed to the exit to leave the bank. Tessa nearly walked into a woman because the woman was looking in her purse instead of watching where she was walking. The woman looked up, and Tessa realized she was face to face with Yvette.

Yvette looked up, surprised. "Tessa, Angela. Hello!"

Tessa and Angie were both surprised to see Yvette. Angie knew she had to think fast and try to get Tessa away from her, but it was too late.

Tessa stood still, staring at Yvette's belly. Yvette smiled and rubbed her small and protruding belly. "How are you, Tessa? I haven't seen you since the funeral. I never got a chance to give you my condolences."

Tessa was speechless and couldn't take her eyes off Yvette's belly. Angela wanted to slap the shit out of Yvette right there in the bank, but she didn't want to go to jail. She grabbed Tessa's arm and led her out of the bank without saying another word to Yvette. Once they got into the car, Tessa broke down and cried. She wasn't sure why she was crying, but she felt so sad all of a sudden. It just wasn't fair. Angie reached over and hugged her sister. "Tessa, please don't cry."

Tessa sniffled. "It's not fair."

Tessa abruptly stopped speaking as if a lightbulb had gone off in her head. Angie got nervous. She knew her sister wasn't stupid, and she knew exactly what she was thinking. Before she knew it, Tessa jumped out of the car and was on her way back into the bank. Angie got out and ran behind her sister, yelling, "Tessa, wait! Not here! This is not the way, Tessa. Please come with me so we can go somewhere and talk!" Tessa stopped in front of the bank. Angie caught up to her and was breathing hard. "Tessa, let's not do this here. Not in front of the establishment where we conduct our business."

Tessa rolled her eyes at her sister. "Angie, if it were you, what would you do? If you had been through everything I've been through, what the hell would you do?"

Angie sighed in frustration. "Okay. I got your back."

Tessa nodded and patiently waited for Yvette to walk out of the bank. After about ten minutes, Yvette came rushing out of the bank, talking on her cell phone. She was so deep into her conversation that she hadn't noticed the sisters following her to her car.

When she ended her call, she went to open her car door when Tessa spoke up, scaring Yvette. "So, Yvette, I guess congratulations are in order. When are you due?"

Yvette turned around and looked at Tessa, a smile playing along her lips as she held her belly. Yvette thought a moment before proudly speaking. "We're expecting our little boy to make his appearance in about four more months. We're so excited."

Tessa stepped closer to Yvette and looked her in the eyes. "Who. Is. We?"

Yvette stepped back a little. "Look, Tessa, I know you've been through a lot, I guess that's why everyone wanted to wait to tell you, but I think us bumping into each other like this is a sign that it's time that you know."

Tessa raised her eyebrows. "And what is it that I should know, Yvette?"

Yvette looked her in the eye with a serious look. "That Edward Charles Thompson will be making his appearance in 4 months, and I don't want any shit out of you or your sister here."

Tessa reached up and slapped Yvette so hard that she fell against her car. Angie grabbed Tessa and held her back. "Oh shit, Tessa! You weren't supposed to hit the bitch! Come on. We have to get out of here!"

Tessa looked at Yvette and spat in her face before letting her sister lead her back to the car. They walked as quickly as they could, hoping no one would call the cops on them. They could hear Yvette screaming behind them, but the two sisters paid her no mind-- they jumped in the car and sped off.

They both were quiet for a minute before Tessa finally spoke, "Maybe I should go and turn myself in, Angie."

Angie placed her hand on her sister's leg. "No, we're going to Mommy and Daddy's house. I'm about to call Sam and--"

"No, don't call him. I don't even want to look at him right now. Angie, I feel like I'm about to lose my mind." Tessa reached into her purse, took out two more pain pills, and grabbed her bottle of water. Angie watched as her sister popped the pills into her mouth and washed them down with some water.

Feeling concerned, Angie started questioning her sister. "Tess, are you in pain? Do you want me to take you to the doctor?"

Tessa shook her head. "No. The pills will start to work in a minute. If you wouldn't have stopped me, I think I could have choked that bitch."

Angie looked over at her sister. "I know, and that's what scared me. I had no idea you were going to slap her. I wanted to, but with her being... well, you know."

"Yeah, I know. And what was she saying about everyone wanting to wait to tell me? Did you know, Angie?"

Angie was scared to answer Tessa's question but answered anyway. "Yes, I knew. We found out on the day of the funeral. We just didn't want you to have to deal with anything else at the moment. We weren't trying to hide it or deceive you. It's just that something like that can send a person over the edge alone, and you were already dealing with stuff. Please don't be upset with us. We were trying to protect you."

Tessa took a deep breath. "It seems like every time someone tries to protect me by keeping secrets. It always ends up hurting me. I guess this family will never learn."

Angie agreed. "I know, Tessa, and I am so sorry."

Tessa looked out of the window. "Yeah, so am I."

# CHAPTER 25

Yvette got herself together and reached for her phone. She dialed Charles, and when he answered, she yelled into the phone. "Your bitch just assaulted me, and she is going to jail tonight!"

Charles was confused. "Yvette, what the hell are you talking about now? Look, I'm working, and I don't have time for your drama today."

This pissed Yvette off even more. "Oh, you're going to listen to what I have to say, motherfucker. I just saw that bitch Tessa at the bank, and she assaulted me. Then she and her bitch ass sister ran off like two fucking punks!"

He was still confused. "Yvette, what are you talking about? Tessa is nowhere near Norfolk or the Tidewater area."

Yvette got in her car and started to drive to her and David's drop-off point at the park. "I'm in Richmond, and I ran into them at the bank."

He was even more confused now. "What the hell are you doing in Richmond?"

Yvette immediately regretted calling him when she realized what she had done. "I, um, wanted to go to some shops I heard about here to shop for the baby."

Sam was furious. "Fuck, Yvette, you just never quit, do you? I've been doing every fucking thing you asked as far as the baby is concerned. All we asked was for you to wait before Tessa found out about the baby. But you just had to fuck that up. What's with your crazy ass? Did your parents drop you on your fucking head when you were a baby? I swear, you are just a fucked-up individual! What the fuck was I thinking when I started fucking with you? Maybe I'm fucked up in the head, too!" Yvette was about to respond, but he disconnected the call.

She didn't have time to worry about them-- she was running late for her drop-off, and she needed to hurry up and get there. After she dropped off the money for David, he called her to check in. She was in no mood for him or his shit today, either.

"Hey Ma, what's going on? My homeboy said you were running late today, and you didn't look so good."

Yvette rolled her eyes and thought *as if he really cared*. "I had a little run-in with Tessa at the bank today-- she hit and spit on me when I told her about the baby."

David burst out laughing. "What the fuck?! You need to learn how to bob and weave, Ma!" Yvette was quiet. She didn't find the situation funny at all. David noticed her silence. "Don't be mad. When you drop your load, you can go after that bitch. This could be good because she is gonna cuss that nigga out and kick his ass to the curb, and that will be your chance to make your move."

Yvette sighed. "Well, I have to give him some space. When I called him to let him know what she did, he cussed me out. I'm on my way to the police department. I'm having her ass locked up."

David yelled. "What the fuck you call and snitch to him for? And now you going to the police? Bitch, take yo ass back to Norfolk and wait for your next move. You so busy operating in yo' feelings, you gonna have both of our asses locked up. The first thing they gonna want to know is why you banking all the way in Richmond."

Yvette yelled back at him. "I could tell them I wanted to do some shopping."

David sighed and spoke slowly and carefully. "I see why you lost your man to Tessa. You don't have a bit of common sense in that pretty head of yours. They're investigating everything that has anything to do with Tessa. If you pull her in the police station, they are going to try to put some pieces of the puzzle together. They have nothing right now, and they're trying to build a case. Take yo stupid ass back to Norfolk and keep yo' fucking mouth shut. Also, if you get that bitch locked up, your parents is going to kick your dumb ass out. They warned you not to tell her, didn't they?"

Yvette responded softly. "Yeah, they did."

David sucked his teeth. "Look, I can't even talk to you anymore today. Do what the fuck I told you, and I will holla at you tomorrow. I need to go smoke a blunt or something-- your dumb ass just got on my nerves." He disconnected the call, and Yvette headed back to Norfolk. She didn't listen to David when he told her to head home-- she drove to Erica's house.

# CHAPTER 26

Angie and Tessa walked into her parent's house and were greeted by their mother. She ran up to Tessa and wrapped her arms around her. Tessa hugged her mom and tried to blink back her tears. She was so tired of crying.

Elizabeth led Tessa to the couch and sat down beside her. "Baby, I know it feels like your life is in a tailspin, but trust me when I say this storm will pass. I promise you, baby. Just try to stay strong."

Tessa sniffed, leaned over into her mother's arms, and closed her eyes. "Mommy, I'm so tired-- you have no idea. I feel like I'm losing my mind. I didn't mean to hit and spit on Yvette-- I just blacked out. If Angie wasn't with me, I don't think I would have stopped hitting her. I'm scared." She sat up and looked her mother in the eyes. "Do you think I'm crazy, Mommy?"

Elizabeth pulled her daughter back to her. "No, Tessa, you're not crazy; you're human. I don't condone violence, so don't tell your Daddy I said this, but I think somebody should have slapped that child a long time ago." They all laughed. It was the first time they were able to laugh in a long time, even though it really wasn't a laughing matter. Elizabeth stopped laughing and looked at Tessa. "Tessa, you need to talk to Sam. You two need to figure out how you're going to handle this. If you plan to go forward with your relationship, there needs to be a plan and some boundaries in place. It's not going to be an easy road. Regardless of how terrible that child is, that baby still deserves love and attention. I know you may not want to hear that, but you need to figure out if that is something you can deal with right now."

Tessa took a deep breath and was quiet for a few moments. Her mother was right. She really needed to have a talk with Sam to make some sense out of the whole thing. She pulled out her cell phone and walked out of the room. Her mother and sister didn't say anything because they already knew who she was about to call.

Sam answered her call on the first ring. "Tessa, I've been trying to call you."

Tessa cut him off. "I know, Sam. And I know why. I'm sure Yvette has already called you. Do I need to come up with some bail money?"

Sam paused. He was caught off guard by her calm demeanor. He thought she would be hysterical like Yvette. "She mentioned pressing charges. I think I might have made it worse when I went off on her."

Tessa was surprised. "Why did you go off on her?"

"I'm just tired, Tessa. I know I haven't made the right choices in the past, and I know that I've hurt a lot of people, but she has to take responsibility for her actions and grow the hell up! I'm just tired, Tessa. We've lost our baby, and she continues to stir shit up all the time. I'm sick of her."

Tessa listened to Sam's rant, waiting for him to finish. "This is only the beginning. She's having your baby, and you will have to deal with her."

Sam didn't know how to take Tessa's tone. He chose not to address the subject anymore on the phone-- instead, he changed the topic. "Where are you? I know that we really need to talk."

Tessa was calm when she responded. "I'm at my parent's house. I'm going to get Angie to take me home, and you can meet me there."

Sam agreed. "Okay, and Tessa, please know that I really and truly do love you."

Tessa didn't reciprocate with an *'I love you'* like she usually did. "Okay, I will see you soon."

Tessa walked back into her parents' den and looked at Angie. "Can you take me home? I need to deal with this as soon as possible. Mommy, if the police come looking for me, just send them to my house."

Elizabeth got up and hugged her daughter. "Tessa, don't talk like that. I'm just waiting for Ed and Maggie to return my call. I called them as soon as Angie called and told me what had happened. They're not going to let that child have you locked up."

Tessa kissed her mother and gave her a strange look before walking out of the house.

# CHAPTER 27

Erica walked into her bedroom and saw Yvette sitting on her bed, crying. She hurried over to her friend and put her arm around her. "Diva, what happened? Why are you crying?" Erica was already stressed out. Phil had showed up at their door today, demanding to see Faith. He had a court order in his hand and the police with him. She contacted her attorney, and he said she had to let the baby go with him for a visit until they could iron things out. Faith had been gone for three hours, and Phil would not answer her calls. According to the court order, he had until 8:00 pm to bring her back, and she had been watching the clock all day. Maybe listening to Yvette and her drama would take her mind off of what was going on with her.

Yvette sniffed and went on about how she was attacked by Tessa and how Charles cursed her out when she tried to tell him what happened. Erica listened but didn't say a word. She really hoped and prayed that her friend would change her ways. It would make life so much easier for her. She prayed for this change every day, hoping her pregnancy would give her a new outlook on life, but it hadn't happened. Erica got up and went into the bathroom, wet a washcloth with warm water, and gave it to her friend to wash her face. Yvette smiled. "Thank you, Erica, you're the only one who cares about me. I can't even go to my parents because I know they somehow are going to blame me for this."

Erica smiled and rubbed Yvette's back. "Are you hungry, sweetie? Let me get you something to eat. The cook is gone, but I can go out and get you some of your favorite wings while you lay here and get some rest."

Yvette looked at Erica with gratitude. "Really? Because I haven't had a chance to eat since this morning, and I know that's not good for the baby."

Erica got up and grabbed her purse. Yvette looked around. "Where is Faith?"

Erica frowned. "She is having a court-ordered visit with her father. He decided to pop up to pick her up for a visit."

Yvette looked surprised but not really concerned. She was too consumed with herself, as usual. She lay back on Erica's bed. "I really do appreciate you, Erica. You're all I have right now." Erica smiled and walked out to her car.

Just as Erica pulled out her phone to give Rome a call, he called her first. She answered. "I was just about to give you a call."

Rome was speaking low. "I have to speak low and quickly, something happened, and I wanted to give you the heads up."

Erica responded. "I already know. She is at my house. I'm on my way to get her some food. I used that to get out and call you. What is going on, Rome?"

Rome took a deep breath. "E, I'm not sure of all the details. All I know is your girl called Sam, all upset about a run-in she had with Tessa and her sister. She said Tessa assaulted her, and she was going to have her arrested. The next thing I knew, Sam went ape on her ass. I mean, he cussed her slam out. I was proud of my boy."

Erica shook her head and didn't respond to his last statement. "This whole situation is getting really out of hand. There needs to be some order and peace for the sake of everyone, especially the baby."

When Erica said the last part, she felt a pang of guilt. She knew the baby wasn't Sam's, and she felt as if she was playing a part in Yvette's game. She just didn't know what to do. If she revealed what she knew, Yvette could get locked up for a really long time. Rome interrupted her thoughts. "Enough about them. How are you doing? Have you heard from your husband since the last time we spoke?"

Erica couldn't help but smile. He was always concerned about her, and he respected her situation. "No, not yet. He has until 8 p.m. with her. I'm just hoping he returns her. He is ignoring my calls on purpose."

Rome agreed, "Yeah, we men can get petty at times. I'm sure he will bring her back on time. Try not to worry. I will text you later to check on you. And good luck with dealing with your friend."

Erica smiled. "Okay, talk to you later."

She smiled at the thought of Rome. He was really a great guy. Not at all like what Yvette described him to be. She had to figure out how to help Yvette clean up this mess so that everyone could live in peace and harmony. She also had to figure out how to clean up this mess with Phil. He was making it very clear that he was not going to quietly go away.

He was, of course, Faith's father.

# CHAPTER 28

Tessa walked into her house, and Sam greeted her at the door. He had been staying with her since she got out of the hospital. He took Tessa in his arms and hugged her tightly. Tessa hugged back, but she didn't say a word. He led her to the couch so they could talk. He sat beside her and began to explain. "Baby, I know you're tired of me apologizing and making excuses. All I can say is that I fucked up again. After we had stopped seeing each other, I had it in my mind that I was going to marry her. She began initiating sex, and I went along with it. I'm not blaming her, but I used to have to practically beg her for sex, and now she was willing and ready to do anything."

Tessa interrupted. "Please spare me those details, Sam."

Sam held up his hand. "My bad. I guess I was being a man. Hell, I don't know, Tessa. She always used protection and made sure it was in before we did anything. She stressed to me right after the engagement that she did not want children until after we were married for a few years. I was shocked when she told me. Again, I'm not putting all the blame on her or making excuses, but I thought we were over." Tessa looked Sam in his eyes just to see if she could detect any ounce of deception, and she couldn't.

"Sam, when and how did you find out?"

Sam took a deep breath. "I found out the same day you got hurt. She met me at the house. I swear, I had no idea she was going to be there, Tessa. She said the neighbor also called her about the sprinklers. She showed me the test. I told her I needed to go with her to the doctor to confirm, and I got out of there. I called Rome to pick you up to meet me so you wouldn't have to wait around much longer, and the rest just went south."

Tessa sat quietly, staring at Sam, but she said nothing. He didn't know how to read her. He took her hand. "I know this is a lot to take in, and I want us to be together-- more than anything in this world. I just feel like instead of making you happy. I keep bringing you pain and grief. Just when it seems like we take a step forward, we take two steps back. I don't want to keep hurting you, Tessa. I love you so much. I want to make you smile, not cry."

Tessa finally spoke. "Sam, I know that you love me, but sometimes love is just not enough. We have tried and tried, but sometimes we have to know when to step back when things get out of control, and that's how I feel right now: out of control. I attacked my pregnant half-sister today and spit on her. I've never wanted to spit on anyone before in my life. The more we fight to be together, the more she fights. It seems like fate is fighting us, also. We lost our child-- his killer is still out there. You're having a baby with a woman you don't love, and she's my sister. It's just too much for me right now. I'm not even sure of what I am capable of doing from one minute to the next. I need some time, Sam. We need to give this a rest, and if it's meant to be, we will be together. I don't think I can handle being around when the baby is born. It's just too much. I am so tired of everything. I miss my baby. I miss being happy. I want to be happy again, but I'm not sure if being with you is the way to go about it. I hope you understand."

Sam stood up, walked over to the window, and looked out of it. He was trying to figure out what to say to make Tessa change her mind. The truth of the matter was he wasn't sure if he could make it without her in his life. She was his life. But how could he be selfish and say that to her right now? It sounded like she was fighting for her sanity, and his issues were threatening it. He knew he had to respect her wishes-- giving her some space and time. He also needed to take that time to try to figure out how to deal with Yvette. He wished he had never met her. Regardless of how he felt about her, she was having his baby and, once again, the only blood relative he had. He had to figure out how to protect his son and not let his mother poison his mind.

He turned around, walked over to Tessa, and pulled her up to her feet. He kissed her deeply and hugged her. "I love you with all of my heart, Tessa-- because of my love for you, I will respect your wishes. The boutique is almost done, and the guys can handle the rest, with Rome overseeing everything. I won't be able to handle seeing you and not being able to be with you. Please call me whenever you need me. I'm going to pack up my belongings and get out of your way."

Tessa sat on the couch and watched him disappear down the hallway and into the bedroom they shared to pack up his belongings.

# CHAPTER 29

When Erica returned, she noticed Phil's rental was in their driveway. She was so excited to see that her baby was back. When she walked in, she noticed that he and Yvette were laughing in the kitchen while Yvette was holding Faith.

She walked in and placed Yvette's food on the table. "Mommy's baby is back!" She took Faith out of Yvette's arms and planted kisses all over her baby's face. Faith giggled and enjoyed the love she was getting from her mother.

Yvette laughed. "I see somebody missed their baby today. I was just talking to Phil. He was telling me about all the interesting job opportunities in Dubai. I'm surprised you never ventured out and tried to spread your wings, Erica. Sounds like there's a lot of money to be made in the marketing field, and Phil seems to have a lot of connections."

Erica gave her friend a blank look. She couldn't believe this heifer was flipping on her like this after all she had been doing for her. She flashed a fake smile, ignoring Yvette's remark, and turned to Phil. "Did you two have a nice visit today?" Regardless of how she felt about Phil, she wanted to remain cordial for the sake of the baby.

Phil gave her a one-word answer. "Yes." He turned to Yvette. "Well, it has been a pleasure talking to you, Yvette-- if you decide to take me up on my offer, give me a call. I will connect you with the right people and with the right direction and drive. You will become successful. All you have to do is want it badly enough."

Yvette got up and gave Phil a hug. "Thank you, Phil. I will definitely keep that in mind."

Phil walked over to Erica and rubbed Faith's curly hair before kissing her on her chubby cheek. Faith giggled and squirmed. Phil looked at his wife with a blank look on his face. "I will be leaving on Friday. My attorney will be in touch with yours in reference to everything. I'm sure you will be happy with the results." Erica nodded and walked out of the kitchen to take Faith upstairs to give her a bath and put her to bed. Once she got upstairs, she ran the bath for her baby and proceeded to give her a bath. She was pissed at Yvette for even entertaining Phil.

Erica felt as if Yvette should have stayed as loyal to her as she had been to her, keeping her awful secrets and everything. She couldn't help but feel betrayed by her friend.

Once Faith was all clean, she gave her a bottle while rocking her to sleep. Faith was out in a matter of minutes. Erica laid her baby down and turned around to Yvette, who was standing behind her rubbing her belly. Erica jumped. "Damn, Yvette, you scared me!"

Yvette smiled. "Sorry, girl! That food was so good! Thank you so much. You're a lifesaver."

Erica mumbled, "No problem, that's what friends are for."

Yvette sat on the bed. "I had a good talk with Phil. I can understand why you found him charming, and he has a lot of connections. I don't know Erica; I think I would have stuck it out and tried my hand at having a marketing career over there. Maybe you wouldn't have felt so lonely and neglected. There are a lot of opportunities over there, and maybe you just didn't give it a chance. Then again, after talking to Phil, he's really not your type. You love those thuggish, blue-collared street guys. So, you guys weren't really on the same page. That's why he might have been trying to groom you to his level when he tried to tell you how to dress. And as far as the young girl, he's an older man-- things like that flatter them when young girls are attracted to them. You know that firsthand."

Erica spun around and looked at Yvette. "Excuse me? What the hell do you mean, 'his level'? And are you insinuating that I'm the reason the marriage didn't work? I'm the reason for the abuse?"

Yvette held up her hands. "No, sweetie. That's not what I'm saying. It's just that he was willing to give you the world, and you don't come across men like that very often. He is very hurt about the way you up and left him."

Erica put her hand on her hip. "So, you discussed me with him, Yvette? After everything I told you? You felt the need to discuss me with my estranged, cheating, abusive husband?"

Yvette stood up and walked over to Erica. "Look, Erica, I'm your friend, and I want what's best for you and Faith. You don't want to end up in the same situation I'm in. That's all I'm saying. Faith is a beautiful, sweet baby, and she deserves to have her father in her life. That's not really possible with him living in Dubai. She needs both sets of grandparents in her life too."

Erica was appalled. Who did this bitch think she was trying to tell her what to do with her child when her shit was all fucked up? She walked up to Yvette. "First of all, I would appreciate it if you let me handle my business and you worry about yours. Because at the end of the day, my baby and I will be just fine. The fact that you entertained that bullshit that Phillip was feeding you makes me question your loyalty to my child and me. I don't need you to tell me what's good for my baby or me. I've got this under control. And for the record, I am a very smart, strong, independent, attractive woman *with* common sense. I don't need a man to validate me or to tell me how to dress or act. I know my worth, and I don't have to put up with any man's bullshit or abuse just so he can take care of me. I'm not going to settle or stay in anything that doesn't make me feel good. I can walk! I have my own money and a degree, and I can build a career right here in Virginia-- or anywhere else, for that matter. I don't have to lie, cheat, steal, manipulate, or sell my soul just to achieve happiness. I am good, and so is my baby."

Yvette put her hands on her hips, "Is that a shot at me, Erica? Are you throwing what I've told you in my face?"

Erica sighed. She was mentally tired from dealing with Phil, and she was exhausted from dealing with Yvette and her issues. She just wanted to take a bath, sit on the phone with Rome and talk until they fell asleep. She walked over to her bed and sat down. "Yvette, it's really been a long stressful day for me. If you want to stay, you can sleep in the guest room. I need time alone to unwind."

Yvette became offended. "No, Erica, it's cool. I can leave. You know, I'm your friend-- I love and care about you. I know this is about the fact that I hit it off with your husband, and you can't get along with him. I know it seems like he is more my type than yours, and that might be true, but you're my girl. I can give you some pointers on how to make it work with him."

Erica had had enough of this bitch. "No, Yvette, I've seen what you do to keep a man, and I'm not built like that. Do me a favor and see yourself out. I'm going to take a bath. Drive safely." Erica walked into her bathroom, closed the door, and locked it, leaving Yvette standing in the middle of her bedroom floor looking and feeling stupid.

# CHAPTER 30

Tessa invited PI Mason over to her home for him to give her an update on the case. She no longer had to meet him elsewhere since Sam was no longer with her.

Mason informed her that he had talked to someone that stayed next door to the house that David had been living in, and with some compensation, the neighbor told him about a woman who would come over almost weekly to the house. The neighbor had seen her come out of the house looking disheveled on many occasions. The neighbor didn't know the make of the car she drove, only that it was fancy and white. But that was months ago, and since then, no one had been in the house, and the police had been around on several occasions asking about David and the roommate.

Tessa sighed. "I feel like we just keep running into one dead end after another. I have just had a rough week. There's also a possibility that I might end up locked up for assault, so I'm going to pay you now, just in case."

Mason looked at her and raised his eyebrows. "Why would you be going to jail?"

Tessa looked away and took a deep breath. "I assaulted my pregnant half-sister when she told me that she was pregnant by Sam."

Mason mumbled, "Damn." He felt so sorry for Tessa. This woman had been through so much, and it seemed like she just couldn't catch a break.

"She came to your home to tell you something like that?"

Tessa shook her head and responded. "No. I literally ran into her coming out of the bank. I noticed her stomach, and she was glad to give me the news. It all went downhill from there."

The investigator side came out of Mason. "In Norfolk?"

Tessa shook her head. "Right here in Richmond."

Mason frowned and looked at Tessa. "Why was she banking in Richmond?"

Tessa shrugged her shoulders. "I have no idea." Mason thought for a moment before he pulled out his pen and pad and wrote something down. Tessa looked at him curiously. "Does that mean anything to you?"

Mason didn't know what to say because he didn't want to get Tessa all riled up, but he needed more information about her half-sister. Tessa had already told him the story about how they met, so he knew he had to tread lightly. He didn't want Tessa to have false information. "Tessa, can you provide me with a picture of your half-sister?"

Tessa raised her eyebrows. "Why? Do you think she had something to do with this?"

Mason continued to write on his pad. "I don't. I just want to cover all bases. Also, what is the make, model, and color of the car she was driving? Do you remember?"

Tessa thought for a minute. "To be honest, I really can't remember. I was so upset, and I just don't remember."

Mason looked at her and smiled. "That's okay. That's easy to find out. I would really like a picture if you have one."

Tessa thought for a moment. She went to her laptop and pulled up Yvette's Facebook page. She found Yvette's profile picture posing in front of her white Mercedes. She lost her breath when she saw the picture and handed the laptop to Mason. He looked at the picture and shook his head. He had a feeling he knew what all of this was leading to. Tessa suddenly felt very cold. She sat on the couch and wrapped her arms around herself.

Mason placed his hand on her arm. "I know how you must be feeling right about now, Tessa, but we can't jump the gun on this. I have to make sure everything checks out, and then we can go to the police. We don't want to act prematurely because she is pregnant, and we don't want you to look like the bad guy."

Tessa didn't respond. She just nodded her head. She was ready for him to leave her with her thoughts. She agreed that they needed to make sure first because if

Yvette had anything to do with her baby dying, that bitch was going to die right along with David. She had no intention of going to the police with this information.

# CHAPTER 31

Yvette walked into her parents' house, trying to be very quiet. She had been doing a good job of avoiding them for weeks. Just as she was about to sneak up the stairs, her mother called her from the den.

"Shit." Yvette walked into the den, trying to look as sad as possible. Her mother started in on her first.

"Come have a seat, Yvette. You already know what this is all about." Yvette walked over to the couch and plopped down, looking at the floor. Her mother continued speaking. "I'm not going to ask you what happened because, frankly, I am sick and tired of your lies. All we asked of you was to stay away from Tessa, and you couldn't even do that. For the life of me, I can't figure out why you were even in Richmond, but there's no telling with you. I just don't even know what to say to you or how to deal with you anymore, Yvette. I know this whole situation is not easy for you, but it's not easy for any of us. That's why we are trying to keep things calm by not having any drama. But you keep on adding fuel to the fire."

Yvette finally spoke, attitude lacing her tone. "So, it's okay for her to put her hands on me?"

Ed spoke up. "No, it's not. And her parents have called-- Tessa regrets doing that, but at the same time, why would you provoke a person who is unstable and mourning? Do you need counseling?"

Yvette had heard enough. "Why is it that we have to tiptoe around her? I'm pregnant now! Doesn't anyone care about how I'm feeling or my health? It's like I'm all alone going through this! You all treat me as if my pregnancy is a curse! Like you all wish that I wasn't even pregnant! How is that supposed to make me feel? It's bad enough that I'm pregnant by a man who is in love with someone else, but I also have to deal with my parents looking down on me. I didn't create this situation alone, you know."

Maggie looked at her. "You didn't create it alone, but you're damn sure the ringleader, Vette! And don't try to run that guilt trip on me because I know you! Like I said before, something ain't right, and I'm going to find out what it is sooner or later. Now you hear me, and you hear me good gal, keep your narrow ass out of Richmond and away from Tessa. If you don't mean her any good, then stay the hell away from her. And no, you will not be pressing charges against her either."

Yvette sighed. "Is that all? I'm really tired, and I need to go to bed." Maggie and Ed nodded. Yvette stood up and marched up to her room like a little child that had just been scolded by her parents.

She got up to her room and called Charles to remind him of her doctor's appointment tomorrow. He picked up on the first ring.

"Hey, baby daddy, I just wanted to remind you about my doctor's appointment."

Sam sighed. "Look, I may not be able to make it tomorrow. I have to take care of some things."

Yvette frowned, "I know you're not putting Tessa in front of your baby's needs."

Sam was quiet for a moment. "You don't have to worry about that anymore. Me and Tessa are over. But I'm sure that was the plan when you magically appeared in Richmond."

Yvette was stunned-- did Tessa really dump him? Yvette smiled. "So, you're going to go off on me and blame me for that, too, huh? Even though she assaulted me while carrying your child."

Charles responded, "Look, I will try to make it tomorrow, but like I said, I have something to take care of first." He disconnected the call. Yvette looked at the phone and laughed.

The perfect ending to a shitty day.

# CHAPTER 32

Tessa left her doctor's office feeling upset. Things had not gone as she had planned. Although she explained to her doctor that she was still feeling pain, he did not prescribe any more narcotics for her. Instead, he told her to get some over-the-counter meds-- he said that they should help to make her comfortable. He was concerned because the amount he prescribed for her should have lasted 30 days-- he said he could not legally prescribe anymore. He also warned her that taking such pills so often could result in an addiction.

Tessa felt anxious and nervous. She felt a dull ache in her back, so she headed to the pharmacy to try to get some over-the-counter medicine to help with the pain.

Once she made her purchase, she got into her car, took two pills, and headed to the boutique. After taking the 30-minute drive, the pills had not helped her any. She was walking slowly into the boutique when her sister noticed her.

"Hey girl, you're moving kinda slow. What did the doctors say?"

Tessa walked past her sister towards her office. "I might have to find another doctor. I told him about my pain, and he refused to give me any more Vicodin. I took some Ibuprofen, as he suggested, and it's not working, Angie. I can't work through the day like this. I really need something stronger."

Angie followed her sister into the office. "Well, Tessa, why would he refuse to give you more meds if you told him you were still having pain?"

Tessa became agitated. "Because he's an asshole! Talking about how I should have had pills left because the amount he prescribed was supposed to last me 30 days, and my last visit was only two weeks ago. He doesn't know my pain, and how dare he tell me how I should feel."

Angie walked over to her sister and rubbed her back. "Calm down, Sissy. Why don't you give the Ibuprofen a chance to work and call back tomorrow if it doesn't help? You can go home, and I can handle things here. It seems like you need some rest."

Tessa rolled her eyes, got up, and grabbed her purse. Her back was really hurting, and she was starting to sweat. She hadn't had a pill since last night, and she was starting to feel really bad. She walked to the door before quickly addressing her sister. "Okay. I will call you later, Angie."

She walked out of the door without waiting for Angie to respond. She got in her car and headed home. She knew she wasn't going to make it through the night with this pain. She stopped at Walgreens on the way home and purchased some nighttime Ibuprofen. She popped two of those as soon as she got back into her car. When she arrived home, she took a shower, lay on her couch, and went into a deep sleep.

Around 2 a.m., she began to dream. She was walking in the hospital, and her baby was crying. She ran down the hallway, checking each room, looking for her baby. "Don't worry, Sammy! Mommy is here! I will find you." She opened each door in the hallway but couldn't find her baby. Just as she got to the last door in the hallway, it opened, and there stood David holding her baby in one arm and a gun in the other. She ran up to him to grab her baby, screaming, "NO! DON'T DO IT!" He held the gun to her baby's head, and she heard it go off.

Tessa sat up and screamed. Once she looked around, she realized she was dreaming and began to cry. She was sweating profusely, and her back was aching. She got up and went to the refrigerator for a bottle of water. She checked her phone and noticed several missed calls from Angie and her mother. She didn't even hear the phone ringing.

Popping two more pills, she walked to her bedroom, lay down, and waited for them to work.

When the pills didn't take effect, Tessa started thinking aloud. "I have to figure out how to get some more Vicodin or something. This is not working for me."

# CHAPTER 33

Yvette sat in the penthouse suite of the Omni hotel enjoying room service. She was eating lobster-- it was delicious. Phil sure knew how to treat a lady. Erica was nuts for leaving him. She picked up her glass of lemonade, wishing it was wine.

"Phil, thank you so much for this lunch. I'm having a great time."

Phil looked at her, smiling. "I'm glad you're enjoying yourself. Some women just don't appreciate the finer things in life."

Yvette laughed. "Are you referring to Erica? I still can't believe she went off on me the way she did. I was only trying to tell her the truth. You are a good man, Phil, and I just want what is best for her and Faith."

Phil smiled. "Do you really? I only want what's best for my daughter. At this point, Erica is no longer my concern. I tried to provide her with a good life, but she is obviously not refined or classy enough to recognize the finer things in life, unlike you, Yvette. That's why I wanted to talk to you. I have a proposition for you."

Yvette blushed and rubbed her belly. Phil walked over to her and began to massage her shoulders. Yvette moaned. "Ah, that feels so good, Phil. Tell me all about it."

Phil continued to rub her shoulders. "I need your help. We both agree that Faith needs her father. In Dubai, I have custody of Faith. I need you to help me take my daughter back to Dubai. If you help me, I will give you one million dollars."

Yvette's body stiffened, and she tried to turn around to face him, but he wouldn't let her. "What do you mean? How would I be able to help you get Faith? I told you about the argument we had. I'm not even sure if she trusts me anymore."

Phil reached his hand down into her dress, and he rubbed her swollen breast. At first, Yvette stiffened up, but it felt so good she moaned some more. Phil bent down and kissed her neck. "I'm sure you are very resourceful, Yvette. I did my homework before I offered you the job. I know about the guy you've been giving money to and how you pawned jewelry for cash. I also know that he is wanted by the police for killing your nephew and shooting your half-sister."

Yvette felt like her heart had stopped. She jumped up and looked at Phil. She felt like she was going to have a heart attack. Phil held out his hand and smiled. "Don't be frightened, honey. Your secret is safe with me. I just want your help. With the money I can give you, there may be a chance that you can pay that guy to disappear forever. If I make him disappear, you and your baby can live in luxury for the rest of your lives. I've been watching Erica and everyone she's associated with since she left. I know everything about everybody in her life, even the guy she is fucking. You don't have to answer me right now-- think it over."

Yvette raised her eyebrows. "The guy she's fucking? What guy is that?"

Phil smiled. "Charles's friend Rome, but I'm not surprised because he's more of her type. She doesn't possess the class you have, nor can she appreciate a good man." Yvette felt her whole body get warm. How could Erica sleep with the enemy? Phil grabbed her hand and directed her to his bed. "Lay back." He commanded. Yvette did as she was told. He pushed up her dress and spread her thighs. He was surprised to see that she wasn't wearing any panties. He inhaled her scent and licked her wet spot. Yvette began to squirm and moan. He put his finger inside her and let it slide in and out. Yvette was in heaven. She screamed and came so fast it shocked her. He removed his fingers and stood up. She struggled to sit up because she wanted more.

"What happened? Why did you stop?"

Phil looked at her and sat beside her on the bed. "I don't want you to think of me as a monster, Yvette. I think you're a beautiful, smart, refined, and classy woman, but we do need to settle our business first."

Yvette placed her hand on his. "I will come up with a plan to help you, but I need you to help me get rid of David. Then we have a deal."

Phil smiled. "Consider it done."

Yvette removed her hand and placed it on his dick over his pants and started rubbing it. Phil moaned, stood up, and took off his pants. Yvette sat on the edge of the bed, reached out, grabbed his dick, and put it in her mouth. It wasn't as big as David's or Charles's, but it would do.

It took him a while to get hard, but she was able to get the job done. He moaned, and when he was about to cum, he pushed her back and sprayed cum all over her dress. "I'm so sorry, honey. I didn't want to do that in your mouth."

Yvette looked down at her dress in horror. "Oh, my God! How am I going to go home like this?"

Phil pulled up his pants, walked to the bathroom, came back with a bathrobe, and handed it to her. "Here, put this on, and I will send your dress to be cleaned."

Yvette took the robe. "Let me rinse it out first. I don't want them to see what kind of stain it is." She hurried to the bathroom and soaked the dress. Since it was a cotton maxi dress, it was easy to wring out.

When room service came, they put the dress in a plastic bag, and Phil paid extra to have it cleaned right away. Yvette sat on the bed admiring Phil's power and money. He looked at her. "Again, I apologize for that. You have to let me take you shopping to make up for your dress."

That made Yvette smile. She jumped up, put her arms around him, and kissed him deeply. She had a feeling that this would be the best business deal of her life.

# CHAPTER 34

Tessa arrived at the boutique the next day, and she felt awful. She didn't get another minute of sleep after that awful dream. The PM pills had her groggy, and her back was still aching. She called the doctor's office to complain, but after he insinuated that she might have developed an addiction, she quickly hung up on him. He didn't understand her pain, and she needed to find a new doctor quickly.

In the meantime, she had an appointment with a potential client, and she needed to get herself together. She walked in, and her sister immediately noticed Tessa-- she had lost a significant amount of weight, and it was starting to show because she was still trying to wear the clothes she had before her weight loss.

Angie approached her carefully, fearful that she may go off on her. "Good morning sis. Are you feeling better?"

Tessa forced a smile. "A little. I know you guys tried to call, but I was sleeping."

Angie nodded. "We figured that. Your appointment will be here soon, and I have the paperwork ready just in case she wants to place an order."

Tessa nodded and walked into her office. She really needed something for her pain. She put her head in her hands and took some deep breaths. She heard someone at her door, and she looked up-- it was Calvin.

"Good morning. Ms. Tessa. Are you okay? I was going to pick up coffee for everybody. Do you want me to get something for you?"

Tessa thought for a minute and looked at Calvin. "Yes, Calvin, I can use a vanilla latte. After my appointment, I would like to talk to you for a moment." Calvin looked concerned. Tessa held up her hand. "Don't worry, sweetie. You're not in trouble or anything."

Calvin exhaled. "Oh, okay, I will be right back with your drink." Tessa made it through her appointment, and the client was excited about Tessa designing an evening gown for her. With that out of the way, she went to search for Calvin, who was sweeping outside of the store. She called for him to come back to her office. When he arrived, she told him to close the door and to have a seat.

Tessa looked at Calvin. "First of all, I would like to commend you on the exceptional job you're doing. You are really living up to our expectations."

Calvin smiled. "Thanks, Ms. Tessa."

Tessa smiled. "Calvin, I'm sure you know what happened to me-- with the shooting and all."

Calvin nodded. "Yeah, that was crazy. I'm just glad you're okay. You are okay, aren't you?"

Calvin noticed her eyes getting watery. Tessa got a tissue and wiped her eyes. "Well, yes and no. I am in a lot of pain, and my doctor is out of town. I ran out of my pills, and I've been trying to take over-the-counter pills until he returns, but they're just not doing the trick." Tessa looked at Calvin to see if he was following her. She felt uncomfortable, but she continued. "I was wondering if you could help me out, Calvin, since you know a lot of people that sell a lot of things. I would pay you, and I don't want you to do anything but direct me to the person. I would go and get them myself." Calvin looked at her and raised his eyebrows. "How about two hundred dollars if you can get me something for my pain?"

Calvin smiled. "As a matter of fact, I do know someone. I can get them for you."

Tessa stopped him. "No. All I want you to do is send him to me. Send him to the shop, and here is your two hundred dollars." She handed him the money. "Can you get him to come and see me today?"

Calvin sat and thought for a minute. "I can see him this evening and tell him to stop by tomorrow. How many do you want?"

Tessa felt anxious and thought for a minute before replying, "Can he get me a hundred? And I really need them today."

Calvin looked shocked. "I'm sure he can, but that's going to cost you. I would have to leave early to go see if I can find him. I can text you when I talk to him."

Tessa nodded in approval. "And Calvin, this stays between me and you. Okay?"

Calvin smiled. "Ms. Tessa, I ain't no snitch. You helped me, and now, I'm going to help you. I want you to feel better. Don't worry. I got you." He walked out, happy about the quick money he had made.

# CHAPTER 35

Yvette's phone rang, and she picked up immediately. It was David. She hadn't heard from him in a few days, and she was anxious to talk to him. "I was wondering when you were going to call me!" She said excitedly into the phone.

David laughed. "Don't tell me you missed me."

Yvette laughed alongside him. "I have some good news. I'm about to make some big money, but I might need your help."

David grunted, "What you talking about, Ma? How's my seed?"

Yvette cringed and quickly answered. "The baby is fine." She hated when he reminded her that she was carrying his baby. Yvette sat on her bed and put up her swollen feet. "A friend of mine needs me to help him out. He's rich and doesn't live in this country. I can't go into details over the phone, but he is going to pay me a lot of money to help him. He has already paid me half, meaning I have some extra to give you."

This information piqued David's interest. "How much money you talking about?"

Yvette smiled. "Let's just say we will be set for life, David. I have five hundred thousand dollars to split with you now."

David muttered, "Shit." He was quiet for a minute before saying, "This sounds big. I need you to come to see me so we can talk more about it face-to-face."

Yvette panicked. She did not want to see David, but she knew she could not back out. "Okay."

David paused. "Cool, let me get with my man and set things up. I will hit you back up with the details." He disconnected the call, and Yvette exhaled. She knew what she was about to do was dangerous, but she needed to get out of this mess she created. An hour later, David called her back with the details-- she would see him tonight with an overnight bag.

Later that night, she drove to Richmond, to the same location where she had met him before. Only this time, a guy who only went by the name of Tee pulled up beside her in a black Lexus with dark windows. He helped her out of her car and made sure she locked it up. Once inside his car, he asked her for the money. She handed it over to him, and he secured it in his trunk. When he got back in the car, he looked at her. "Buckle up." She reached over and did as she was told.

They rode for almost an hour, turned off of 95 North at the Fredericksburg exit, and went down several dark roads. She looked at her phone, and she had no signal. She was surprised he hadn't taken it from her. She felt pressure on her bladder and really needed to use the bathroom, but she didn't ask. She just wanted to get to their destination. They arrived at a house that was isolated with a lot of trees around it. Tee looked at her, "You can get out." She got out of the car and looked around, but it was hard to see anything because it was so dark. She followed him up the walkway to the door. He knocked and waited. Someone peeped out of the curtains at the window, and a moment later, the door swung open.

Tee stepped aside and allowed her to walk in first. She walked into what looked like a living room with only a couch and television. She turned around at the sound of David's voice. "Hey, Ma. Wow, you getting big!" He walked up to her and kissed her, shoving his tongue in her mouth. As usual, her body reacted to him. She pulled away when her bladder reminded her that she had to go to the bathroom.

She smiled. "David, I really need to go to the bathroom."

He looked at her and smiled. "Okay. Follow me." He led her down the hallway to a half bathroom. It was clean and very small. She closed the door and took care of her business. Once she was done, she opened the door and found her way back into the living room. Tee was gone, and it looked as if it was just her and David. She walked over to the couch as David sat quietly counting the money that he got out of her bag. She waited patiently for him to finish counting.

He smiled. "Good job, Ma! So, tell me about this plan you have."

Yvette cleared her throat. "Well, my best friend Erica's soon-to-be-ex is trying to take her baby away from her. I convinced him that I was on his side and that I would help him take the baby back to Dubai. He has already paid me this advance as a show of good faith."

David frowned. "How the hell did you manage to convince him of that?"

Yvette smiled. "I said all the right things to him. He thinks that I am angry because Erica is dating Charles' best friend, Rome. He thinks I want to pay her back."

David looked at her. "You mean that nigga I shot?"

Yvette exhaled. "Yeah, him. They apparently have been sneaking around, and her husband had her followed. Phil has a lot of money and resources. He has already offered to set me and the baby up for the rest of our lives if all of this works for him."

David became really interested. "Really?"

Yvette nodded. "Yes, but this is the issue. He also had me followed, and he knows about us--"

"FUCK YOU MEAN HE KNOWS ABOUT US?!"

Yvette jumped and began to feel nervous. "Apparently, when Erica left him, he had her, and everyone associated with her followed. I told you he was very rich and resourceful. He made it his business to tell me that he knew you shot Tessa and Rome. He said he could make it all go away if I helped him. It was almost like blackmail."

David sat down and thought for a moment. "Did you tell him you were meeting me tonight?"

Yvette shook her head. "No."

David walked over to the window. "Shit, Yvette, why didn't you tell me this shit before you came here?!"

Yvette tried to stay calm. "It doesn't matter. If he was having you followed, he already knows where you are, David. Don't you get it? All he really cares about right now is getting his baby away from Erica."

David shook his head. "Yeah, and when we help him do that, he will fuck us. This money was just bait, Ma. He is using us, and then he is going to turn on us. Trust me."

"Well, what are we going to do?"

David's phone went off, and he looked at it. "Give me a few days to come up with something, and I will get in touch with you. Tell him we accept his offer. Let me figure this shit out. My man, Black, is coming to take you back to Richmond tonight. I need to set some things up, and I don't need you distracting me."

Yvette looked surprised. "You told me to pack an overnight bag."

David looked at her and shook his head. "Yeah, I know, but the plans changed. Black will be here in a few. Go home, and I will call you in a few days."

There was a knock on the door, and David peeped out the window and opened the door. This tall, muscular dark-skinned man walked in, followed by this very attractive tall, brown-skinned woman.

The woman was very slender with curves in all the right places-- she could have been a model. She wore black leather pants with a sheer leopard print blouse and a lacy black bra underneath. She stood tall in her black, red bottom stilettos. Her hair was silky black and hung straight down her back. What really got Yvette's attention were her eyes. They were grey and shaped like a cat's eyes. They were beautiful, but Yvette could see evil in them.

Yvette couldn't help but stare.

The pair walked in, and David did the introductions. "Yvette, this is Black, and he will be taking you back to Richmond."

Yvette smiled and said her greetings. Black held out his hand to shake hers. "Nice to finally meet you, Yvette."

David cleared his throat. "And this is Cat."

Yvette forced a smile and held out her hand. "Hello, nice to meet you, Cat."

Cat looked at her. "So, you're the one he knocked up?"

Yvette was caught off guard-- she didn't know how to respond. Cat looked at Yvette's hand and walked past her to sit on the couch. David stared at Cat as he spoke to Yvette. "Look, Yvette. Black is gonna take you back now. I have a lot to do tonight."

Cat looked over at them, rolled her eyes, and opened her Chanel purse. She took out a baggie that contained weed and proceeded to roll up a blunt. David went over and picked up Yvette's belongings and ushered her out of the door with Black.

On the ride back to Richmond, Black talked the whole way. Yvette tried to engage in the conversation as much as she could, but her mind was racing. She couldn't get Cat off her mind and was trying to figure out what her relationship was with David. She also couldn't figure out why it was bothering her so much. She thought about asking Black but decided against it. She was sure he would not give out any information.

Instead, he went on and on about his interest in real estate.

# CHAPTER 36

One week later, Erica walked into her parent's house like she was on cloud nine. She had, once again, had a wonderful date with Rome. He was perfect in her eyes; she never wanted their dates to end, and he acted as if he didn't want them to end, either. Her parents agreed to babysit Faith so that she could get out of the house and have some adult time with Rome. Their hearts went out to her for all that Phillip was putting her through. She was so grateful for the time alone with Rome.

She walked into the house, and it was completely dark. She called out to her mother, but she didn't get an answer. She turned on the lights and walked up the stairs to the room she shared with Faith. She figured they were up there and had probably fallen asleep. When she walked into her room, she let out the loudest scream. "OH MY GOD, MOMMY!!" She yelled as she ran over to her mother who was lying on the floor with her eyes open. As she got closer, she noticed the blood on the front of her mother's blouse. She screamed again, jumped up, and ran over to Faith's crib. It was empty. She ran from room to room, screaming and crying. "FAITH, DADDY!!"

When she realized that her baby was gone, she fell down on her knees and began to cry. She ran over to the kitchen and dialed 911-- just as she was about to speak into the phone, she looked over and saw her father lying on the floor with his throat slashed. She let out the most horrific scream. She began to shake all over.

The voice of the 911 operator brought her out of her spell. She mustered up enough strength to whisper. "Please, help me, my parents are dead, and my baby is gone." She was so frantic; she could barely tell the operator what had happened. She hung up and called Rome. "BABY, PLEASE COME BACK! IT'S FAITH. SHE'S GONE!! SOMEBODY TOOK MY BABY!! AND I THINK MY PARENTS ARE DEAD!"

# CHAPTER 37

After Tessa met with the guy for her pills, she immediately took two-- her body instantly relaxed. Just as she was about to doze off at her desk, her phone rang-- it was Mason.

"Hey, I didn't expect to hear back from you so soon."

Mason responded, "Hi, Tessa, I really didn't expect to get all I needed so soon, but I think I have everything you've been looking for. I'd rather not go over this by phone. Can I meet you at your house in about an hour?"

Tessa felt butterflies in her stomach, along with the effects of the pills taking over her body. She took a sip of water before she spoke, "Yes, that will be fine." She hung up the phone, grabbed her purse, and hurried to her car to meet him.

Tessa stepped out into the cool air and took a deep breath. Her head felt heavy, but she kept moving. She did not want to miss her meeting.

She drove home carefully because she did not want to be stopped with the pills with no prescription. Once she made it home, she staggered into the house and decided to lie down and wait for Mason to get there. She must have fallen asleep because she was startled by the sound of the doorbell ringing.

She jumped up, and the room started spinning. Her heart was beating fast, and she could barely stand up. She grabbed onto the couch and shook her head, trying to get her bearings. The doorbell rang again.

"Just a minute!" She slowly walked to the door while leaning against the wall for support.

When she opened the door, she noticed the surprised look on Mason's face. She immediately became conscious of how she must look. She ran her hand over her hair and tried to straighten out her maxi dress.

"Are you okay, Tessa?" Mason waited for her response with a look of concern.

Tessa opened the door wider to let him walk in. "Yes, just a little tired. I don't get much rest with everything that's going on, you know?"

Mason walked in and nodded. Once seated in the living room, they got down to business. Mason pulled out his pad and began. "So, me and my people went back out to David's last known residence and showed his neighbor the picture of your sister and her car. She confirmed that she was the one seen coming to visit David on several occasions. I asked if she told the police this information-- she hadn't. She stated that they never asked about the comings and goings of other people. They had only asked about the people living in the house."

"With the new information, we trailed Yvette a few nights ago from her home back to Richmond. She got into a vehicle with this man." Mason handed Tessa a photo. "After handing him a duffle bag, they drove off to a deserted road in Fredericksburg. They went into this old house that looked as if it was abandoned. She went in with another guy and stayed for about two hours. During the time she was in the house, another vehicle pulled up, and a tall attractive female got out, along with another guy, and walked into the house. After a few minutes, your sister emerged from the house with the gentleman, and we caught a quick snapshot of David standing at the door."

As Mason spoke, he showed her pictures of everyone and everything he witnessed. Tessa sat in total shock as she listened to this man tell her how her half-sister helped her ex-boyfriend kill her baby.

Mason waited a few minutes, giving Tessa a chance to digest everything he had told her. "I know this is a lot to take in at one time, but at this point, I really think that you should get the police involved and to try and catch this guy. Don't wait too long because it seems like he is not staying in one place very long. I have everything you need to know written down in my report, along with the pictures." Tessa nodded, but she had an odd look on her face. Mason sat next to her and put his hand on her arm. He really felt bad for her. "If you want, I can go with you to the police."

Tessa shook her head. "No, I'm okay. I really appreciate all you have done for me. You have no idea what all of this means to me."

She reached over and gave him a hug. He was caught off guard, but he hugged her back. He really felt for Tessa and what she was going through-- Mason was a detective for the Fredericksburg Police Department that lost his wife as a result of a suspect wanting revenge. That was too much for him to bear, so he took early retirement. He later decided to open up a PI firm to help other victims whose cases ended up getting lost in the system due to the high crime rate in Richmond.

Tessa and Mason released each other, and Tessa looked at him as if she was seeing him for the first time. He was actually attractive. He had a pretty brown complexion with soft wavy hair that was cut short and broad shoulders with a muscular frame-- he also smelled really nice. She was extremely aware of how she must look and was embarrassed by her appearance. "I'm sorry, Mason. You must think I'm really crazy."

Mason looked at her and put his hand on her hand. "Not at all, you've been through a lot, and I commend you for keeping it together this much. I just want you to get justice so you can live your life. And call me Derrick."

Tessa blushed, but she had no idea why. "Thank you, Derrick, for everything you've done. I will be able to handle everything from here. I will go to the police in the morning with all that you have given me. If you don't mind, can you continue to follow those two until I can get the police involved?"

Derrick raised his eyebrows. "Well, I would think they would immediately get on it once you present them with everything you have."

Tessa looked away and didn't respond. Derrick was experienced enough to know all too well what Tessa had on her mind. He was starting to care about this woman, and he didn't want anything to happen to her. He didn't let on that he knew what she was thinking because he didn't want her to lose trust in him.

"Tell you what, I will keep my people on them until the end of the week. I know this is a lot for you, and that will give you some time to digest everything and let your family know what is going on."

Tessa looked at him with a smile of relief. She hugged him again. "Thank you, Derrick."

He hugged her back. He held her back, looked into her eyes, and kissed her gently on the forehead. "So, we have a plan."

Tessa smiled. "Yes, we do and thank you again. When this is all over, you have to let me treat you to a meal or something."

Derrick looked at her, stood up, and smiled. "Are you asking me out?"

"It sounds like it, doesn't it?" Those pills really had her feeling good, along with the realization that she was about to avenge her baby's death.

Derrick pulled her to her feet and kissed her hand. "When this is all over, I will take you on a date, beautiful." Tessa stood there smiling. She didn't know what else to say.

Derrick walked towards the front door, and she followed. He opened the door, turned around, and hugged Tessa. She wrapped her arms around him and took in the clean scent of his cologne. "I'll be in touch, beautiful. Lock up and have a good night."

# CHAPTER 38

Sam sat in front of Tessa's house and couldn't believe his eyes-- how could she have moved on so fast? And who the hell was this dude?

Sam felt sick to his stomach. He was coming by to check on her and make sure she was okay, but it looked like she was doing just fine. Suddenly, he became angry. "Man, fuck her!" He hit his steering wheel, and he felt his eyes beginning to tear up. His life kept getting worse.

Just as he was about to pull off, his phone vibrated. It was Yvette. "Yeah?"

Yvette sighed. "Well, hello to you too, baby daddy. I was just calling to let you know that I have a doctor's appointment in two days. They said there is an issue with my bloodwork, and they need me to come back in."

Sam took a deep breath, trying to keep calm. "What do you mean, Yvette? Are you doing everything that you're supposed to be doing?"

Yvette became upset and started to cry. "Why do you automatically blame me for everything? Do you really think I would do something to hurt my baby? I am doing the best I can, considering the circumstances, and no matter what anyone thinks, this baby is innocent in all of this."

Sam felt bad for being so hard on her. "I'm sorry, Yvette. I just have a lot on my mind. I will go with you to the doctor and make sure we both are doing what we can to make sure you and the baby are okay."

Yvette smiled. "Thank you, Charles. That's all I really want."

"Look, have you eaten today?"

"I ate some fruit earlier, but I've had such a busy day trying to get my affairs in order, trying to find a place to live. You know my parents gave me a moving date, and that hasn't changed even with the news of their new grandchild coming."

Sam felt guilty again. He didn't want his child to be homeless, and he knew that Yvette really didn't have any means of income. "Don't worry about all of that. I will get a place for you to live and set up a nursery for the baby. If you're up to it, we can go looking tomorrow."

Yvette felt excited. Her plan was beginning to work. She smiled and tried to sound sad. "Okay. If that's what you think is best. Thanks so much, Charles. I'm glad you're stepping up for your son. Call me in the morning, and I will be ready. I really need to get off the phone and try to go get some food. Ethel is gone for the day, and I don't think there's anything cooked."

"I will bring you some food. I'm in Richmond, so it will take me some time to get there. I will just stay in a hotel, and we can leave together in the morning to go looking for a place."

Yvette grinned. "I'm sure my parents won't mind you staying in their pool house, Charles. Call me when you're close. Thanks!"

Sam pulled off and headed to his apartment to get some clothes, then got onto I-64 and headed to Norfolk to take care of his baby's mother.

What had his life become?

# CHAPTER 39

Yvette was ecstatic when she hung up the phone. She danced to her closet, trying to find something to wear that was sexy but not too obvious for Charles's arrival. Things were finally falling into place for her.

Two hours later, she was at the pool house when Charles knocked on the door. She opened the door and smiled. Charles looked at her and smiled as well, but he looked sad and as if he had lost some weight.

Their baby would fix that-- he just had to see it first. His happiness would come back for sure, and he would forget all about Tessa.

"Hi, baby daddy!" She said as she pulled him into a hug. Sam didn't hug her back. His hands were full of bags of food and his overnight bag. He walked in and sat everything down, "I got you some Chinese food. I hope that's good."

"Anything is fine, considering I haven't had anything but fruit today."

He smiled. "Okay, have a seat on the couch. Look in the other bag; I rented some movies. Put a movie on, and I will make our plates."

Yvette smiled. "Okay, cool, this is like old times. Movies and Chinese food. This was your favorite thing to do after you had a hard week at work, remember? I would always be upset because I wanted to go out on the town on Friday nights, but now, I think I would appreciate this."

Sam smiled. "Good-- change is good sometimes. I think we all are starting to change."

Yvette agreed and walked over to him. "I really mean it, Charles-- I have had time to think about all that's gone on. After everything that happened, I know I should have done things differently. The recent events have really been a wake-up call for me. I don't know what I would do if something was to happen to our baby. I know you don't believe me, but my heart really goes out to Tessa. I know this isn't the ideal situation, but our baby is coming, and he is innocent. I just don't want him to be forgotten about or to feel unloved by his father."

Charles put his hand on Yvette's stomach-- he felt the baby kick. Yvette laughed. "See, he knows his daddy already."

Charles smiled and suddenly felt the need to protect and take care of both Yvette and his son. He wasn't about to let the same thing happen twice. He refused to lose another child.

He looked at Yvette and searched her face for any deceit or deception-- never taking his hand off of her belly. She looked so beautiful. Her face had filled out, and she had her hair pulled back in a ponytail without any makeup on. She looked so natural and innocent. Charles rubbed her belly. "Don't worry. I will be here for you and our son, Yvette. You and he will not have to worry about anything."

Yvette smiled and hugged him tightly. This time, he hugged her back. She pulled back and looked into his eyes, and he bent down and kissed her on her lips. She opened her mouth and slipped her tongue into his mouth. While they kissed, their hands began to roam each other's bodies. Yvette pulled him towards the bedroom, and he followed. Once in the bedroom, Yvette reached for his shirt and began to undress him. Charles stood there and let her. Once he was naked, Yvette pushed him onto the bed and took off her dress-- she didn't have anything on underneath it. Charles looked up and admired her pregnant body. He reached for her. He needed human contact so much at this moment. He laid her down and began to kiss her belly. Yvette moaned and opened her legs.

Charles looked up. "Let's hold off until after you see the doctor. Let's just lay here and hold each other for now." Yvette started to protest, but she agreed.

Their moment didn't last long. Charles' phone kept going off, and so did hers. Then, her parents were at the door knocking frantically. They both hurried to get dressed and went to see what was going on. Charles opened the door, and Mr. Duncan was standing in front of him, looking upset. "Charlie, you and Vette get over to Erica's house. Something terrible has happened."

# CHAPTER 40

Rome held on to Erica, but she was inconsolable. The police were all over the house. They tried to answer the detective's questions to the best of their ability, but there was just too much going on. The police officer asked them if there was anywhere they could stay that night because the whole house was considered a crime scene, and they could not be there for a couple of days.

At that moment, the Duncans were finally allowed in. Mr. Duncan immediately told them to come to their home. Erica refused to leave. She thought maybe someone might come to bring her baby back. She had given the detectives all the pictures she could find of little Faith in hopes that the police could find her precious baby.

The detective asked her about the whereabouts of Faith's father, and Erica's eyes turned very dark. "That bastard has my baby. This is all him." She began to cry. "Y'all have to find him before he leaves the country with my baby!" She was hysterical again. Rome put his arms around her and explained the situation to the detectives. She went to her parents' living room, took out their wedding picture, and handed it to the detectives. "If he takes my baby to Dubai, I will never get her back!" Erica didn't even know where he was staying. The detectives asked them to calm down and let them do their jobs-- the detective then informed them that they really needed them to clear out of the house.

When they walked outside, Sam and Yvette pulled up together and ran toward them. Yvette grabbed Erica and hugged her tightly. "Diva, I'm so sorry-- what are the police saying?"

Erica pulled away from Yvette. "Nothing. Absolutely nothing. And that motherfucker can be on his way to Dubai with my baby! He KILLED MY PARENTS!"

Erica started to cry again, and Yvette held on to her. She nearly dropped to the ground herself when Erica blurted out that her parents were dead. "You think it was Phillip?" Erica looked at Yvette like she was crazy, "Who else would want my baby? Really, Yvette? Did he really fool you that much?"

Yvette tried to back down, "No, I'm just saying that all of this is really extreme. I mean, why would he hurt your parents?"

Erica looked at Yvette and rolled her eyes-- she had the nerve to talk after all the shit she pulled?

Just as she was about to say something else, Sam walked over and gave her a big hug. "Don't worry,

Erica. They will find him and your baby. Just let me know what you need me to do, and consider it done."

Erica nodded. "Thank you so much. I know how you feel now, and I don't wish this on anyone."

Sam rubbed her back. "Hey, you have to know that's not going to be your outcome."

Erica thought about her parents, and her eyes began to water. Yvette was listening closely and wanted to be sure Erica didn't slip up and reveal too much to Charles. She walked over. "You all can come back to my parent's house for the night."

Erica looked at her and stared for a minute as if she wanted to say something to her. "No, I'm going with Rome. I have to get out of this neighborhood." Erica felt pain in her chest and broke down again.

Rome put his arm around her and looked at Sam. "Um, we need to talk, homie. I will be giving you a call when I get a minute."

Sam already knew what the talk was about, so he nodded. "Okay."

# CHAPTER 41

Tessa sat quietly in the Fredericksburg woods. There was no movement in the house, and it was dark. She had been waiting for over an hour, and there was no sign of David. She thought to herself that she would give it another hour, then she would come back and try again tomorrow.

Hopefully, he hadn't changed his location already. She was really hoping to kill two birds with one stone and catch that bitch Yvette here, also.

A dark vehicle pulled up-- she couldn't believe her luck. She didn't have to worry about them noticing her. She had on all black, and it was so dark that you could barely see your hand in front of your face. This was the perfect location because it was so far out that she doubted anyone ever came here.

She heard voices, but she couldn't make out what they were saying. She did notice that one was a female. It looked like the female was carrying something, but she couldn't make out what it was. She waited for them to enter the house, and she counted to 20. She put her hood on her head and made her move towards the house, tightly clutching onto her gun with her gloved hand.

She moved quietly up the stairs to the front door. She knocked on the door and moved out of sight. She heard footsteps and a deep voice. "Yo, man, come in. We tryna stop this baby from crying!" That's when Tessa heard a baby. The sound of the baby brought tears to her eyes. What were they doing with a baby? Was that Yvette's baby? She couldn't have had it already.

Tessa shook her head. Her lack of sleep and those pills were starting to take their toll on her. She came here to do a job, and she was going to get it done. She opened the door-- both the female and the man were busy standing over the dirty couch, looking helplessly at the crying baby. The sight of the baby set Tessa off. She raised her gun, and just as the man turned around, she fired three shots into his chest. He fell down immediately. She didn't hesitate or give the female time to react. She fired at her, and she fell down, also. The baby began to scream-- she aimed the gun at the baby but immediately put the gun down.

She walked over to the baby and gathered her up in her arms. The baby began to calm down. She looked down at her victims and realized that neither one of them was who she wanted them to be. She also couldn't figure out whose baby this was. Was it the female she had just killed? She had no time to think things out. She needed to get out of the house. She wrapped the baby in a blanket and exited the house. Just as she was walking down the stairs, she heard movement behind her. She raised her gun to the darkness. She could hear her heart beating in her ears. Just as she was about to fire, a light flashed in her eyes, and she heard a familiar voice.

"Don't shoot, Tessa! It's me! Derrick!"

# CHAPTER 42

Yvette was quiet on the drive back to her parent's house. Charles assumed it was because of everything that went on. Erica wasn't exactly seeking her best friend for comfort, and he wondered what the little exchange concerning Phillip was all about. He made a mental note to ask her about it, but right now, he was more concerned about his baby. He reached over and placed his hand on hers. "Are you okay?"

Yvette jumped at his touch. He looked at her, puzzled. "I'm sorry, I was just in deep thought about everything that's happened. I feel so scared. Why is all of this happening, Charles? Who is doing all of these terrible things to us? What if they come after me and our baby?"

Charles rubbed her hand. "Yvette, that's not going to happen. I will be here to make sure of that."

Just as she was about to respond to him, her phone vibrated from a private number. Her heart began to beat really fast. She knew she had to answer it because it was David. Charles noticed she didn't answer. "You're not going to answer?"

Yvette thought quickly. "It's my mother. I'd rather just go up to the house to see if everything is okay. Can you drop me off there, and I will just come down to the pool house after I make sure they're fine? She just lost her best friend, and I know she is a mess right now. It might be a while."

Charles squeezed her hand and agreed. "Okay, just call me when you're ready to come back. If you're too tired, just stay in your room, and we will figure things out in the morning." She breathed a sigh of relief, thankful that he had bought her story. She leaned over, quickly kissed him on the lips, got out of the car, and hurried into her parents' house.

The house was quiet. She went up the stairs as fast as her belly would allow her to, locked herself in her room, and waited for David to call her back. He had a lot of explaining to do. He wasn't supposed to kill anyone. Just as she completed her thoughts, her phone rang. "What the hell happened over there?"

Yvette was trying to speak as low as possible, but not David. "YO! SHIT IS ALL FUCKED UP! I NEED YOU TO MEET ME WHERE WE PLANNED IN AN HOUR! LET HIM KNOW WE ON THE WAY AND THE PRICE HAS DOUBLED!"

Yvette was confused. That wasn't the plan. She knew not to discuss too much on the phone. "Okay, I will see you in an hour."

Yvette immediately called Phillip. "Hi. We need to meet in an hour. Is that okay?"

Phillip responded, "I'm just leaving the police department. This wasn't in the plan."

Yvette sighed, "Well, some things have not gone according to plan, and our meeting needs to take place in an hour. And the price has doubled."

Phillip paused for a moment. "Okay. Same place?"

"Yes." She disconnected the call. Yvette sent Charles a text:

*I'm going to stay close to my mom. She really isn't taking this well. I will see you in the morning.*

*Ok. I think that will be best.*

She took a deep breath, put on some sweats, grabbed her purse, and headed to the meeting.

# CHAPTER 43

Tessa sat in the back of Derrick's car, holding the baby. She was a nervous wreck. Derrick sent one of his employees to pick up her car as they left Fredericksburg. He assured her that everything would be okay and to just leave everything up to him.

She reached into her pocket and pulled out her bottle of pills. She swallowed two of them dry. She needed to calm her nerves. She looked down at the beautiful baby. Whose baby was this, and why was she in that horrible-looking house?

Derrick got back in the car and pulled off without saying anything to Tessa. She felt like he was in deep thought, and she didn't want to interrupt those thoughts-- as long as he helped her out of this mess.

What was she thinking? She just killed two people. Her mind was so messed up. She began to cry quietly. She didn't want to wake the baby, and she didn't want Derrick to see her crying. She had dozed off, and when she woke up, they were in front of her house.

Derrick got out, opened her door, and helped her into the house. She carefully laid the baby on the bed and made sure she was secure. She walked back out to her living room to join Derrick. He was on his cell phone talking to someone.

When he finished, he looked over at her. "Are you okay?" She burst into tears. Derrick moved over and took her in his arms. She released all the pain she felt. She must have cried for a good twenty minutes. Derrick just held on to her as she let it out. When she settled down, he finally spoke, "Baby, we have a lot going on here. That baby was taken from Erica Collins. She's friends with your sister, Yvette. They took the baby and murdered Erica's parents." Tessa's eyes got wide, and she covered her mouth. Derrick continued, "We have gotten in the middle of some deep shit, Tessa. I'm thinking Yvette was in cahoots with David to kidnap the baby to get more ransom money for him, but something must have gone wrong, and Erica's parents ended up dead. Now we have the baby, and we have to figure out how to get the baby back to Erica."

Tessa looked scared. "What about the other two?"

He held up his hand. "Don't worry. My people have already taken care of that. We just had to wait until David showed up and discovered the baby was gone. He hauled ass after that, so that's when my people went in and took care of everything because we knew he wouldn't be coming back. He's running scared right about now. One of my men is following your sister as we speak. My guess is that she is going to meet David."

Tessa felt sick to her stomach. "So, what are we going to do about the baby?"

"Right now, all we can do is sit and wait, baby. I have surveillance of them taking the baby, as well as you going into the house. I had everyone followed. We just have to see what Yvette and David are going to do. Then, we will contact Erica. Trust me. She will go along with us."

Tessa shook her head. "What kind of evil person is my sister? Who goes around just ruining people's lives?"

Derrick shook his head as well. "I've seen a lot in my career, and I must admit your sister has some deep issues. She's about to land herself in jail."

# CHAPTER 44

Yvette pulled up to the warehouse, where they agreed to meet. She noticed a vehicle was already there. She walked into the dimly lit warehouse, and she felt shivers go up her spine. Her baby was moving so much. She tried to calm him down by rubbing her belly as she walked in. She noticed Phillip standing off to the side in the shadows. "Yvette, where is David?"

She walked over to him. "He called me at home and said we should meet in an hour. He should be here any minute."

Phillip was sweating profusely. "I watched the news. No one was supposed to be killed, Yvette. I hope he doesn't think I'm paying extra for that. We didn't agree on anyone dying."

Just as Yvette was about to respond, she heard David behind her. "No, that's not what we agreed on, but we had to do what we had to do to get the job done, and it will cost you."

Phillip became angry. "That's bullshit, and you know it! You were just supposed to take my daughter and bring her to me safely. Where is she?"

David smiled. "You give me the money, and I will bring her in. If you don't have it with you, I have no problem sending her with her grandparents." Yvette felt nauseous. Her mouth was watering, the baby was kicking like crazy, and she felt weak. She silently prayed that Phillip had all the money.

"Let me see her first." Phillip tried to call his bluff.

David became angry. "Fuck that! I'm not playing games! Give me the money, or forget about seeing that baby!"

David turned to walk out. Phillip held up his hands. "Okay, just don't hurt her! The money is in my trunk-- just follow me out to my car."

David and Yvette trailed behind a nervous Phillip to his car. When they walked to the trunk, David pulled out his gun and held it to Phillip's head. "Don't try anything stupid."

Phillip opened the trunk and pointed to the black duffle bag. David nodded to Yvette to get the bag. They all walked back into the warehouse and waited for Yvette to skim through the money to make sure at least the first amount was there. It was all there with stacks of additional bills left over. She looked at David with relief. "It looks like it's all here."

David smiled. "Good job, baby." That's when he pulled the trigger and blew Phillip's brains out. Yvette screamed and sat on the floor, and covered her head.

She was crying uncontrollably. "Get your shit together, follow me, and don't try no funny shit, bitch."

Yvette got into her car and was shaking all over. She could not believe what she had just witnessed. A part of her wanted to drive straight to the police, but she knew that would only land her in prison, as well, and she could not have her baby in prison.

She followed David for an hour until they ended up somewhere in Petersburg. He pulled up in front of a motel. He walked over to her car. "Go get a room and hurry up."

She quickly got out, but she really had to go to the bathroom. She walked into the motel lobby and asked for a room. After she handed the desk clerk her ID, she asked him about a restroom. When she stepped out, David was standing by the door waiting for her. She jumped back because he scared her. "I had to use the bathroom."

He gave her a strange look and walked back out of the motel lobby. Once she paid for the room, she went back outside and handed him the key. He took the key, grabbed the bag of money, and put his arm around her as they headed to the room. Once in the room, he dropped the bag on the bed, sat beside it, and looked at her.

She stood by the door nervously. She really wanted to leave, but she needed to find out about Faith. "So, where's Faith?"

David looked at her and squinted his eyes. "Who? Oh, you mean the baby. Good question. I got back to the spot; Cat and Black were dead, and the baby was gone. That's why I wasted that motherfucker. He tried to play me."

Yvette couldn't believe her ears. "What do you mean she was gone? Why would he bring the money if he already had the baby? That doesn't make sense, David! My goddaughter is really missing! We have to find her!"

David looked at her like she had lost her mind. "The only thing I gotta do is get the fuck up outta here, and so do you! We don't know what is going on; the best thing for us to do is disappear. We have enough money to do that."

Now it was Yvette's turn to look at him like he was crazy. "David, I'm about to have a baby. I can't just run off. What about Charles? The plan? We have to find Faith. If I disappear, it will look suspicious. My parents would definitely come looking for me. We have to think this through." Yvette felt tears coming to her eyes. This has really gotten out of control, and she was in so deep that she didn't even know what to do. Maybe she should just run off with the baby-- but what kind of life could she provide for him on the run? And what if she was caught? He would be without a mother. Right now, she needed to get as far away from David as possible. "David, why don't you take the money and go? I will stay here to find out what is going on. We no longer have Faith, so I really need to find out who has her. As long as I have Charles, I can keep the money rolling in to you. Just contact me when you get somewhere safe."

195

David looked at her long and hard before he spoke, "Okay, Yvette. I don't have to tell you the consequences if you cross me. I'm taking all of this money, and I will contact you when I think things have died down because I can't live on this forever. Come lay down with me. We both can use some rest, and all of this excitement has made a nigga horny."

Yvette panicked. "I really have to go back. Charles is with my parents, and I don't want them to wake up and see that I'm gone."

David smiled. "Just give me some before you leave. I know you want it."

Yvette felt like she was going to vomit. She walked slowly over to the bed. She figured if she could get it over with, she could hurry back home to safety. She walked over to the bed and heard a loud explosion. Before she knew it, several police officers had busted into the room, pointing guns and yelling for them to get down.

# CHAPTER 45

Tessa paced back and forth in her living room. She was so nervous. She kept going to her bedroom to check on the baby, who was still sleeping peacefully. Once Derrick showed her pictures of Erica and her boyfriend, she realized that she was dating Rome. She immediately contacted Sam and told him to get Rome and Erica over to her place-- it was an emergency involving Faith. She prayed everything would go as planned and she wouldn't end up in jail. She just didn't know if they should share the part she played in all of this with them, but Derrick said it was the only way to get them to trust her. He doubted that they would report her since she rescued her baby.

Tessa went to the bathroom, took two more pills, and washed them down with the water from the sink. When she walked back out, she felt a little calmer.

Derrick walked up to her, looked her in the eyes, put his arms around her, and kissed her deeply. She welcomed his affection. She knew that he put himself on the line for her, and she really appreciated him. She felt like he understood her; instead of judging her, he took charge and helped her.

The doorbell rang, and they looked at each other. Derrick smiled. "Show time." Tessa sat down on the couch while Derrick went and opened the door. Sam and Rome looked shocked when he appeared at the door. Derrick disregarded their looks and spoke. "Looks like everyone is here. Please, come and have a seat. We have a lot to go over." Sam felt angry, but he knew now wasn't the time to express his feelings. Right now, it was about getting Faith back.

He spoke up. "So, you said you had information that would affect all of us?" Sam looked at Tessa; she sat close to Derrick and leaned on him as if he was the only thing holding her up. Her eyes were sad, and she was getting so thin. He wanted to feel sorry for her, but he couldn't look through his anger and jealousy.

Derrick spoke first, "Yes, a few months ago, Tessa hired me to find out the whereabouts of a suspect that shot her, your baby, and Rome. During my investigation, I not only found out his whereabouts, but I stumbled upon a lot more information." He handed the photos of Yvette coming and going out of David's house, photos of them together, as well as pictures of Yvette handing David money.

Sam could not believe his eyes. He was in shock. "Tessa, what is all of this?"

Tessa took a deep breath. "Sam, I wanted to avenge our baby's death. I was mourning, and I just could not get past the fact that my baby, our baby, was gone. At that moment, I felt like no one understood how I felt, so I called Derrick to help me. It ended up being more to the story than I could have imagined. Your ex-fiancé, and present baby mama, set me up. She was in cahoots with my ex-abuser to get rid of me and our baby."

Sam was blown away. He couldn't stop staring at the pictures.

Derrick spoke up. "I also had surveillance of the house in Fredericksburg. Once I realized that Ms. Duncan was involved, I had her followed, also."

He looked at Erica. "This is where you come in, Erica." He pulled out more photos of Yvette going to the hotel, meeting Phillip, and them going out to lunch together.

Erica gasped and shook her head. "That dirty bitch was fucking Phillip?"

Derrick hunched his shoulders. "I don't have any proof of that, but you will find this interesting." He turned on Tessa's laptop and showed them footage of David breaking into her parent's house and then running out with the baby. "They must have placed Faith in a huge duffle bag-- I hadn't realized that the baby was in the bag. I thought it was a robbery, so I immediately called the authorities anonymously when I saw it go down. Erica arrived minutes after I called."

Erica stood up. "So that bastard has my baby?"

Tessa cleared her throat. She couldn't hold it in any longer. She knew how it felt to be separated from your baby. "He did, but when Derrick gave me the whereabouts of Dav-- well, I wanted to go and kill him for what he had done to me. So, I went to Fredericksburg. I wanted to face David and kill him. I went to the house-- this guy and this woman were there, and I saw this baby lying on the couch. It made me think about my baby and what I thought they were about to do to her and I... OH GOD, FORGIVE ME!"

Derrick put his arms around Tessa as she wept. Erica was going into hysterics, as well. "WHAT? WHERE IS MY BABY?" Just as she yelled, Faith started to cry. Erica jumped up, "FAITH? IS THAT MY BABY?" Tessa nodded and pointed to her bedroom. Erica jumped up, ran to her room, grabbed her baby, and began to cry. "OH, MY GOD! OH MY GOD!

Tessa walked into the bedroom and stood watching Erica reunite with her baby. She couldn't help but wish that was the ending to her story. Erica looked at Tessa. "You saved my baby. Tessa, I don't know how to thank you. You saved my baby. I don't know how to repay you."

Derrick summoned them back into the living room. "We still have some unfinished business. There are the details of what went on in that house that enabled Tessa to rescue your baby."

Erica held up her hand. "Look, I don't care if Tessa killed all of those bastards. They deserved it. I have no parents, and they took my baby."

Derrick nodded, "Well, you may not care, but the police are another story. We have to all be on the same page with this."

Erica looked directly at Derrick. "I will tell them whatever you want."

Derrick spoke up. "There's a note being placed in Rome's mailbox as we speak telling the time and location of where to pick up your baby. All you have to do is go to the police with the note and your baby. Tell them you didn't trust them, and the note clearly said no police. Tell them your baby was right in the location stated on the note. They will keep the note for forensic purposes, and we have the bag the baby was carried in."

Erica nodded her head and agreed. She looked at Tessa and Rome and took a deep breath. "Tessa, I know I'm in no position to be striking any deals with you or anything, but since I have a secret on you, it's only fair that I reveal my secret. I feel like I owe you this."

"What are you talking about, Erica?"

"When I came home a few months ago, Yvette came to my house to talk. She told me some things that were going on with her. Yvette and I have been like sisters since we were five years old. We always kept each other's secrets and had each other's backs. I knew I should have said something sooner, but so much was going on with my situation, and things were moving so fast with Rome. I just kept praying that things would work out. She told me all about David and all the things she did to set you up. And how David was supposed to kidnap you for ransom and make you disappear. She didn't anticipate getting pregnant with David's child."

Sam jumped up. "What the hell do you mean? She was fucking that nigga?" Tessa looked shocked at Sam's outburst, but she was just as shocked at what Erica was revealing.

Rome was also in shock. "E, you kept all of that from me? After everything we talked about?"

Erica looked down, and tears started rolling down her cheeks. "I know, and I really wanted to tell you, Rome, but at some point, I felt like knowing all of this made me just as guilty. I was trying to find a way to fix it, but I just wasn't coming up with any solutions. I am so sorry, everyone. Yvette was like a sister to me, and I wanted her to be okay."

Derrick rubbed Tessa on her back. "Damn."

Tessa shook her head. "Secrets will do it every time."

# CHAPTER 46

Yvette screamed at the top of her lungs and put her hands in the air. "Please don't shoot! I'm having a baby! Thank God you're here! I was so scared-- please help me!" The officers ran over to David and jumped on him, cuffed him, and took him away. The officer grabbed Yvette by her arm, and as soon as she stood up, she felt a burst of fluid gushing down her legs. She screamed again, "OH, MY GOD! MY WATER BROKE!"

She began to cry; this wasn't supposed to be happening-- she still had three more months. "Ma'am, please have a seat on the bed while we wait for the paramedics. Are you in any pain?"

Yvette could not stop crying. She shook her head. She just wanted her mother at that moment. The officer spoke into his radio. "We have a pregnant woman, a possible kidnap victim, in distress. Her water just broke."

At that moment, Yvette knew exactly how to play this. She wasn't about to have her baby in prison. She cried some more and grabbed her stomach. The officer instructed her to stay calm. Minutes later, the paramedics came and whisked her off to the hospital. On the way, she gave them her parents and Charles's phone number to meet her at the hospital. Right now, the only thing she wanted to focus on was having a healthy baby. The rest would have to wait.

Once in the ER, she was whisked off to the delivery room. The baby was coming fast, and there was nothing anyone could do about it.

# CHAPTER 47

Three months later

Tessa and Erica pulled up in front of the hospital. They had gotten to know each other in the past three months and found out they had a lot in common. They also leaned on each other for support-- considering both of them suffered traumatic losses at the same time. After explaining all of the craziness to her family, with encouragement and support from Derrick, she admitted to having an addiction to painkillers. She started going to outpatient treatment and talking to a psychologist about dealing with the loss of her baby. She was finally able to see the light at the end of the tunnel, and she started to feel much better.

Derrick took her on a date, as promised, and agreed that they should take things slow. She and Sam agreed to be friends, and he even attended some of her counseling sessions to help them deal with the loss of the baby and the relationship. Erica and Rome decided to slow down on their relationship, as well. Even though he understood her reasoning behind keeping Yvette's secret, he still had to work on trusting her again because she stood by and let Sam and Tessa endure so much pain when she could have just spoken up. He was in love with Erica, but he just needed a moment to make sure she could be trusted. Erica completely understood. She was just grateful that he didn't give up on her completely. She was also seeking counseling to deal with the tragic loss of her parents and her estranged husband.

David was in prison awaiting trial for a number of charges: murder, kidnapping, breaking and entering, grand larceny, extortion, etc. For some reason, he had not tried to implicate Yvette in any of this, and no one seemed to know why.

Yvette lived on pins and needles every day. She was so stressed out. Edward Charles Thompson was born prematurely. Charles kept his word and found a house for her and the baby. Even though he didn't move in with her, he still came around to assist her with the baby at the hospital and made sure he signed Little Edward's birth certificate.

After the baby was born, he had become a little distant, and she couldn't figure out why. Little Edward had been in the hospital for three months, and now he would be going home with his mother because he was finally able to breathe on his own. Yvette looked at her baby and never felt so much love for another individual. Even though her parents were angry with her about what she had done, they still loved their grandson and were excited about the baby coming home. She was so relieved that David was in prison and not naming her. Her part in everything was a secret. She guessed he really didn't want his baby to be born in prison. Now that the baby was born, she couldn't help but wonder if he would start to talk.

Erica had called Yvette the day before, asking if she could come to see the baby. She was so glad that her bestie had come around and was ready to resume their friendship. She knew that Erica had gone through a tough time, and it was her fault, but she never meant for it to go that far. She hoped that Erica would never find out about the part she played in her tragedy. She was finishing up feeding her baby when Erica and Tessa walked in. She was surprised to see Tessa and wondered what they were doing together. She smiled. "Erica, what's going on?"

Erica smiled. "Hi, Yvette. I'm sorry I misled you into thinking that I wanted to come and make amends with you. Actually, Tessa and I wanted to talk to you before you went home to give you some information and a solution to a problem that you have."

Yvette looked at both of them like they were crazy. She stood up and said, "What? You two are friends now? What problem do I have that you all can help me with? Erica, do not tell me my sister has convinced you to feel sorry for her." Tessa decided to take over. She didn't have the time, or the patience, to listen to Yvette's foolishness.

Tessa stepped all the way into the room and closed the door. She looked at Yvette, went into her bag, pulled out a large envelope, and handed it to Yvette. Yvette snatched the envelope. "What the hell is this? What is going on?"

Tessa smiled. "Just open it, and you will know exactly what's going on…Sis." When Yvette pulled out the many photos and looked at them, she felt sick. Her legs got weak, and she involuntarily sat down in the chair. She was at a loss for words. Here she was, thinking that her secrets were locked away with David in prison, but here was everything looking back at her in a pile of photos. She was speechless.

Tessa laughed and spoke, "You know, Yvette. I'm actually in therapy because of everything you put me through. All of this because of a man that didn't want you. And he still doesn't want you. What you have there is your life and what you have become. If I go to the authorities with everything we have on you, you will be placed in prison for the rest of your life. But, since you're my sister, I'm going to look out for you. I'm going to give you an offer you can't refuse. See, you took my baby away from me. You tried to take Erica's baby away from her, and you took her parents away from her. I propose, in exchange for our silence, you sign these."

Tessa went into her bag and pulled out some more documents and handed them to Yvette. She took the envelope, and her hands were shaking. She read the documents and jumped up. The pictures spilled onto the floor. "Are you fucking crazy? You must be crazy if you think I'm going to give you complete custody of my baby!"

Tessa laughed. "Oh no, honey, you will be signing those documents so that I can adopt your baby. I've already been to an attorney to put everything in motion. All you have to do is come with me to a notary downstairs, sign the papers, and I will be taking little Edward home with me. See, either way, you won't have your baby because once I go to the police, they're going to lock your ass up, and you will be in prison just as long as that piece of shit you conspired with." Yvette began to cry.

Erica finally spoke up. "Yvette, I was trying to understand you, but you crossed so many lines. I think you should sign the papers. At least you will be able to see him at family functions. In prison, you may not ever see him again."

Yvette looked at Erica. "Erica, you knew about everything."

Erica agreed, "Yes, and Tessa knows that and how bad I felt about everything. You have no loyalty, Yvette. I was loyal to you, and what did you do? Had my baby taken away and had my parents killed!"

"Erica, I tried to call you so many times to explain to you."

Erica held up her hand. "Just sign the papers, Yvette. It's in your best interest."

Tessa spoke up again. "Look, your secret will be safe as long as you sign those papers and don't try to cross me. You have more to lose than me. You took my son, and now I'm taking yours. You will have to live with the same pain I live with. It's only fair." Yvette looked over at her baby sleeping peacefully and broke down and cried. Tessa and Erica were not affected at all. "Don't worry. We have it all sorted out. We will tell our parents that you decided to live your life to the fullest, and a baby would only hold you back. Don't worry, they will believe it. They know how selfish you are."

Yvette stood still, just staring at the papers. She couldn't believe she was about to lose her baby. "Well, can I take some time and have my attorney look them over?"

Tessa shook her head, "No. He comes home with me today. We have everything set up for him." Yvette's mind was racing. It's either sign or go to prison. She knew they weren't playing with her.

"What are you going to tell Charles? Does he know the baby is not his?"

Tessa spoke up. "Yes, he does, but he is still willing to be in his life. That's why he's still coming around. He doesn't know about this agreement, and it would be in your best interest if you didn't tell him about it either. So, go on and sign the papers, Yvette, and stop stalling."

Yvette started to cry. She had no place to turn. She had done so much, and now she was about to lose her baby. "I need a pen." Erica handed her a pen. Yvette looked at Erica and searched her eyes to see if her former friend felt any compassion for her as a mother.

Erica recognized her look. "Ain't no fun when the rabbit's got the gun, huh?"

Tessa called the notary into the room and requested everyone's Identification. Yvette signed the papers, and the notary stamped them. Yvette walked over to her baby, picked him up, kissed him, and whispered, "Goodbye for now, my precious little boy. Mommy will get you back somehow." She placed him back down into the bassinet and began to cry. "How can you be so cruel?"

Tessa laughed. "Cruel? My first thought was to kill your evil ass, and then my next thought was to send you to prison. I'm letting you walk around free, and you're alive. You should be grateful!"

"This is not over. Believe me, I'm getting my son back one way or another."

Tessa laughed again. "Oh, really? What you really need to focus on is that other lunatic that's in prison-- I hear he is not happy with you. He doesn't know about this deal, but you better pray he gets life, or the death penalty, for what he's done."

Erica cleared her throat. "I'm going to go downstairs and pull the car around to wait for you guys.

Tessa agreed. "Yes, Yvette, you can leave with the baby. We will all walk out together, and you can put the baby in Erica's car so I can take him to his new home.

I have already called a family meeting at our father's house for tomorrow, and we will make the announcement together about the recent turn of events. And don't try to get cute, sis. Just follow my

EMETRICE NICHELE

lead, follow the script, and you will be just fine." Just as Erica walked out, the nurse walked in with a social worker and some discharge papers. Tessa smiled at the social worker. "Good, you're here. Everything has been taken care of."

She showed the social worker the papers, and she looked at Yvette. "I think this is a very noble thing you are doing, Ms. Duncan. So many women just take the babies and just neglect and abuse them. You giving him to your sister is such a kind act."

Yvette stood fidgeting. She really needed to get out of there. "Now that everything has been signed, do you all need me for anything else?"

The nurse looked at the Social Worker, then at Yvette. "No, Hun. You're free to go." Yvette walked out of the room, leaving her precious baby behind. She was hurt and angry, and she didn't want them to see her sweat any longer. She needed to regroup to figure out how she was going to get her baby back and make them all suffer.

# CHAPTER 48

One year later

Tessa looked at her precious little boy, Edward, playing and sticking his hands in his birthday cake. She couldn't believe a year had gone by so quickly and Little Edward was growing so quickly. Even though he was really David's and Yvette's son, that didn't make Tessa love him any less. She looked at Sam right by his son's side, smiling, he loved him so much, and Little Edward loved his daddy. Even though they weren't together, they had agreed to co-parent, and things had been working out very well. They decided to keep the secret that Little Edward wasn't really Sam's baby. Sam even signed his birth certificate. He deserved a normal life with two loving parents, and Sam and Tessa were more than willing to provide that for him.

Tessa and Derrick were going strong. They got along very well and shared a bond. He was really there for her during her toughest time. He was even there for her when she decided to discreetly get outpatient help for her pill addiction. He told her that she would not be any better of a mother to Little Edward than Yvette if she did not admit she had a problem and sought professional help. She did what he said, and she was in a much better place. She felt so complete and happy. Even if this wasn't the ideal family, she felt that she had the perfect family.

Derrick was okay with her co-parenting with Sam. He also understood, and that made Tessa love him even more. Derrick asked her to marry him, but she told him she needed more time, and he understood. Sam was still in love with Tessa, but he accepted their fate. He was just happy that she allowed him to be in his son's life. They were great parents to Little Edward, and he was the happiest baby. It hurt his heart to see her with Derrick, but he focused on his son, and it made things easier for him. Derrick was really an easygoing, nice guy. He had been on such an emotional roller coaster with Tessa, and Little Edward was the only good thing that came out of this. He wasn't aware of the agreement. All he knew was that Yvette had signed over all parental rights to Tessa and left town.

According to her parents, Yvette was in Atlanta, trying to make a life for herself. That was fine with Sam and the whole family. Even though everyone didn't know the extent of the crimes she committed or the trouble she caused, they felt a sense of relief that she was gone. She spoke with her parents once a week to assure them that she was fine. Her father was still sending her an allowance, and he didn't mind as long as she was out of their hair, causing trouble. Her parents loved her, but her decision to move gave them a much-needed break from her and the drama. They were surprised, and her mother was somewhat suspicious of her decision to give her baby to the woman she hated. She just couldn't believe the fact that Yvette had changed so quickly and made this grown-up decision on her own. She let it go because deep down inside, she knew that Little Edward was in better hands with Tessa and Sam.

Erica and Tessa had become very close, also. The two of them had more in common than they realized, and Erica had even started working with her and Angela at the shop. She and Angela were her marketing team.

Rome and Erica had some rough patches after she confessed to knowing what Yvette had been up to, but they eventually got past it and were engaged to be married. Erica and Faith had even moved into a larger house that Rome bought and renovated for them. Erica sold her parents' home because she just couldn't stay in the house knowing what happened to her parents there. She put the money from the sale of the house, some of the money from the insurance policy, and money she inherited after the death of her husband into a trust for Faith. Her in-laws tried to fight her on it, but she was still his wife, and everything went to her because he didn't have a will. After they found out that they had no claims to his money, she never heard from them again. They never even checked on Faith. Erica gave him a small funeral ceremony. That was the last time she saw them, and that was fine with her. She just felt bad that Faith lost her grandparents, but Rome's mother had stepped up and taken on the role of grandma to Faith. Erica and Faith adored her.

Ed Duncan and his wife walked in with their arms filled with gifts for little Edward. "Happy Birthday, lil fella." Ed put the gifts on the floor, walked over, and picked up his grandson. He loved him so much. Little Edward giggled as his grandfather kissed him on both of his chubby cheeks. His wife took the baby out of his arms and showered him with kisses, also.

Tessa laughed and walked over to her second parents and gave them a hug. "I'm glad y'all finally made it."

Mrs. Maggie shook her head. "Traffic was awful. The rain would not let up, but we weren't about to miss our baby's first birthday party."

Tessa's parents walked over and greeted the Duncans. Tessa's mom looked around at their extended family. Everything had fallen into place, and she silently thanked God. She hugged the Duncans. "Now that the whole family is here, we can get this party started."

# CHAPTER 49

David sat on the prison bus and looked out of the window. It was raining like crazy. He was still waiting for his trial, but they transferred him to another prison. He often thought of Yvette and the baby. He tried to contact her, but her phone was out of service. He tried to tell the authorities the part she played in everything, but no one believed him. His lawyer didn't even believe him. He kept talking to him about pleading guilty to lesser charges that would only give him life in prison instead of the death penalty. He was not going out like that.

Yvette had crossed him, and she was going down with him. She hadn't even bothered to find a way to send him some money while he was locked up.

Black and Cat were dead, and they couldn't even find their bodies. They were even trying to pin those missing person charges on him, too. He knew she had the baby by now, and Yvette was probably living happily ever after with that dude. The thought of how she and others had crossed him was making him so mad that he was getting a headache.

The rain was coming down really hard, and the corrections officer driving the bus had swerved twice. The thunder was so hard and loud that it shook the bus. Some of the other prisoners were mumbling out of fear on this bumpy ride.

There was a loud clap of thunder and a sharp flash of lightning. This distracted the driver, and he swerved. The prisoners began to yell. It seemed as if he had lost control of the bus. The bus hit a car, swerved into another car, and began to flip. The bus flipped on the guardrail, began to descend down a hill, and crashed into a tree. David tried to look around, but his head was pounding. He felt something dripping into his eyes, and he knew it was blood. Some of the other prisoners were moaning, and he was sure that some were dead. He maneuvered his way closer to the window. His hands were cuffed, and he tried to locate the corrections officers to see if they were alive. He looked over at another prisoner, a small white guy, and he had his eyes open, trying to do the same as him.

The guy looked at him. "We have to work together quickly." David nodded in agreement.

The guy was smaller, and since the bus had landed upright, he managed to get up to try to kick the gate open that separated them from the driver and the other officer. To both of their surprise, the gate fell open. David got up. His head was throbbing, but he wasn't about to stay on that bus. The other guy looked at the officers. Both of them appeared to be dead. He checked their pockets for the key, and he unlocked his cuffs and David's. When they got off the bus, it was still raining hard, but that didn't stop them from running up the hill. When they reached the top of the hill, they looked at each other, nodded, and ran in opposite directions.

David was on a mission. He had a score to settle.

# TO BE CONTINUED

# ABOUT THE AUTHOR

Demetrice Nichele has been writing short stories, plays, and novels since she was in grade school. Her passion for storytelling is felt through her ability to paint everyday people's intricate and sometimes messy lives on the page.

Demetrice is the mother of two adult children. When not writing, she enjoys serving customers in her baking business, reading, traveling, and cooking.